"Someone wants me dead," Samantha said.

She paused, then continued, "I just need a place to lie low for a while. I don't want to cause any trouble."

John watched her carefully. "Maybe I can help."

"I appreciate that, but the less you know the better."

Why couldn't Samantha trust him?

"If you say so." He took a step toward the door, realizing he wouldn't get anything else out of her. It was her choice, and he could do nothing about it.

"John..."

He paused and looked back. "Yes?"

Samantha's eyes brimmed with tears. "If anything happens to me, will you make sure my son is okay? I just need to know that someone will watch out for him." Her voice cracked.

His heart ached at the vulnerability of her words. "Absolutely."

He paused another moment. He didn't want to leave, and he wasn't even sure why. But his throat squeezed with pressure, and his feet seemed rooted where they were.

Books by Christy Barritt

Love Inspired Suspense

Keeping Guard
The Last Target
Race Against Time
Ricochet
*Key Witness
*Lifeline
*High-Stakes Holiday Reunion
Desperate Measures

*The Security Experts

CHRISTY BARRITT

loves stories and has been writing them for as long as she can remember. She gets her best ideas when she's supposed to be paying attention to something else—like in a workshop or while driving down the road.

The second book in her Squeaky Clean Mystery series, *Suspicious Minds,* won the inspirational category of the 2009 Daphne du Maurier Award for Excellence in Suspense and Mystery. She's also the coauthor of *Changed True Stories of Finding God in Christian Music.*

When she's not working on books, Christy writes articles for various publications. She's also a weekly feature writer for the *Virginian-Pilot* newspaper, the worship leader at her church and a frequent speaker at various writers groups, women's luncheons and church events.

She's married to Scott, a teacher and funny man extraordinaire. They have two sons, two dogs and a houseplant named Martha.

To learn more about her, visit her website, www.christybarritt.com.

DESPERATE MEASURES

CHRISTY BARRITT

HARLEQUIN® LOVE INSPIRED® SUSPENSE

Recycling programs for this product may not exist in your area.

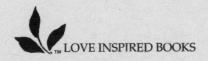 LOVE INSPIRED BOOKS

ISBN-13: 978-0-373-44620-9

DESPERATE MEASURES

www.Harlequin.com

Printed in U.S.A.

I will say of the Lord, He is my refuge
and my fortress, my God, in whom I trust.
—*Psalms* 91:2

This book is dedicated to everyone who likes adventures off the beaten path and long for a place where time has stood still.

ONE

Samantha Rogers looked over her shoulder, trying to maintain her composure in the inky black parking lot. Her heels clicked against the pavement and the overstuffed paper sack in her arm teetered.

Why weren't the overhead lights working out here? Sure, the grocery store was in the middle of nowhere, in Yorktown, Virginia, a town where crime was practically nonexistent. But the soft glow of "Hal's Market" on the sign above her did little to comfort her or guide her steps.

A footfall sounded behind her.

She craned her neck but didn't see anyone. The sound spooked her enough that she quickened her pace. Her shoe caught in a crack, and she nearly toppled onto the asphalt.

She righted herself, but not before an apple escaped from the top of her bag and rolled under a nearby car.

No way was she stopping to retrieve it. Not with the way imaginary spiders scattered across her skin and her throat ached as she tried to hold her fears at bay. Tension pounded at her ears as she strained to hear another telltale sign that someone was following her.

Her paranoia reared its head at the worst times. But Samantha could have been certain that the man in the grocery store had been watching her. His bulging muscles, heavy jowls, and rocklike hands only made him appear to be dangerous. That's what she tried to tell herself, at least.

For that matter, the man was probably shopping for the same household staples she was. She'd stopped by on her way home from a late night at work to grab the usual— milk, eggs, bread and some fresh produce. A lot of people stopped to get those things. That's most likely why the man's movements inside the store had paralleled hers.

He was just someone on his way home. His wife could have called him and reminded him they were out of milk. That was it.

She may have mentally convinced herself that her theory was true, but her body still remained on alert.

Samantha's SUV came into view. It was only four parking spaces away. The heavy downpour earlier had flooded the front of the lot, so she'd had to park in the back. Now she wished she'd battled the ankle-high water closer to the store instead.

With her free hand, she fumbled inside her purse until she found her keys. She grasped them like a lifeline.

Almost there.

Almost safe.

She'd pick up Connor from his karate class, go home and lock her doors.

Then she'd laugh at herself for being so silly. She'd make jokes about her paranoia. She'd tell herself she had an overactive imagination.

Though she tried to brush off her anxiety, it didn't work. How much longer could she live in this fear? It wasn't fair to Connor. Every eight year old should have a stable, predictable life. Connor deserved to live in the same place for more than a few months at a time. He needed a safe place to call home.

This wasn't how she'd imagined her life turning out.

Always looking over her shoulder. Tense. Afraid.

She reached her SUV and rounded it to the driver's side. Relief filled her. That footfall had been her imagination.

As she hit the button to unlock her door, a man rushed from the shadows.

She dropped her bag and tried to scream. Before she could, the man's fist collided with her jaw. The force of the hit propelled her backward, into her vehicle. Her head snapped back, cracking against the SUV.

It was the man from the store. The one with arms that looked like tree trunks. With a neck as thick as his head. Who towered above her by a foot, at least.

She *hadn't* been paranoid.

"Did you think we wouldn't find you?" he mumbled. Spittle showered her, followed by a blast of the man's hot breath. "We always find who we're looking for."

Her knees went weak, and she began sinking to the ground. She didn't stand a chance against this man. Her one hundred and twenty pounds weren't enough. Her cell phone was out of her reach. Her keys jangled as her feet hit them on the asphalt.

This man was going to kill her, and she could do nothing about it.

No, she had to think about Connor. She had to *fight* for him. She couldn't let this man win.

Her gaze quickly scanned her surroundings for something—anything—she could use as a weapon. All she saw were a dozen broken eggs, a busted milk carton and a loaf of bread.

Tears threatened to squeeze out as the man grabbed her blouse and jerked her back to her feet. His fist struck her stomach.

Deep, jarring pain made stars swim before her eyes. Her ribs ached. Air squeezed from her lungs.

"You have some very powerful people looking for you." He pressed her against the SUV. "One in particular said you need to pay for what you've done."

Wasn't there anyone else out here? Anyone to call for help? The SUV formed a barrier, making it impossible for anyone coming from the store to see them.

"Leave me alone," she mumbled, her head spinning. "Someone already killed my husband."

"*Someone* killed him?" He grunted. "You killed him. An eye for an eye."

"Of course I didn't." Her voice cracked.

"That's not what I heard."

"Please. I have a son. He needs me." Maybe she could reason with this man. It was doubtful. But maybe. She didn't have many options right now.

She quickly soaked in the man's features. Gold tooth. Snake tattoo stretching up his neck. She'd never seen him before. He had to have been contracted by someone—one of her husband's former friends.

"I wasn't hired to be compassionate. I was hired to bring you in—dead or alive. Dead would be less of a hassle."

The man punched her in the gut again. The air rushed from her lungs. Tears spilled down her cheeks.

He reached into his back pocket and pulled out something shiny.

A knife, Samantha realized.

Any hope she had for surviving disappeared faster than her last paycheck.

Dear Lord. Help me!

Just then, a siren screeched in the distance. The man startled at the sound.

Adrenaline surged in Samantha. She had to fight for her life. To fight for her son.

Finally, the scream that had been lodged in her throat

escaped. She pushed the man away with a strength that surprised even her. Then she sprinted toward the store.

She ran, not looking back until she reached the inside. There, she sagged against the wall.

She glanced outside, just in time to see the man scowl at her. He climbed into his car and squealed off. She was safe. But for how long?

She had to get Connor and run. Where? She didn't know. What would she do once she got there? She had no idea.

But staying here was not an option.

"I know people think I'm crazy, but I've got to do this." John Wagner leaned back in his chair, not liking the tension across his chest. He'd felt this tension for far too long now. "I've got to make some life changes. I've been in denial about it for a long time."

"I think it's a good choice," his friend Nate said. "Even if people think you've lost your mind." His friend grinned as he leaned against an empty table in The Revolutionary Grill. It was Tuesday night, the one night of the week the grill didn't open. That's why John always stopped by, every week on the same night, to hang out. Nate and his wife owned this place.

Today would be John's last visit for a while, though. In the morning, he'd leave for Smuggler's Cove where he would begin a new adventure. He'd worked at the Coast Guard Training Center here in Yorktown for the past five years.

Now it was a time for a fresh challenge: restoring nine cabins on the remote island of Smuggler's Cove, located in the middle of the Chesapeake Bay. John was looking forward to some new scenery and new faces. Mostly, he was hoping his soul might be restored right along with the old cabins.

Since Alyssa had died, nothing in his world had felt right. This life change was his last-ditch effort to find some peace, to make things right with himself. He prayed to God that would be the case. If this didn't work, what would?

Finally, John took his last sip of coffee and stood. He raised his cup in acknowledgment of all the Tuesdays he and Nate had done this. "As always, thanks for the coffee. You guys will definitely be what I'll miss the most about this place."

"We'll be out there to visit you in a week," Nate added. "Work fast."

"You know how to put the pressure on, but there's no one else I'd work as hard for." It was the truth. Nate and his wife Kylie had been loyal friends to him. He'd do anything for them.

Just then, the back door of the restaurant flew open. John's gaze traveled through the kitchen, swerving in the direction of the sound.

A woman stood in the back entrance, her eyes wide. Blood trickled from her forehead, her lip was busted, her gaze looked frantic.

Nate rushed toward her, his eyebrows furrowed together in worry. "Samantha? Are you okay?"

The woman nodded and touched her forehead.

That's right, John realized. It was Samantha, the woman who was renting the room above the restaurant. He'd hardly recognized her in her disheveled state.

John had seen her around a few times. She was hard not to notice with her trim build, soft blond hair that fell to her shoulders and the mysterious air about her. She kept to herself, but her gaze was always searching her surroundings, as if she was on guard or looking for someone.

She'd spiked John's curiosity, but that was as far as it had gone. Ever since Alyssa, John knew he didn't deserve the chance to even consider a relationship. Besides, Samantha seemed like a closed book, someone whose body language screamed, "Keep your distance."

John joined his friend, scanning for trouble out the backdoor window. Before he even reached Samantha, he could see her trembling.

"I'm fine," Samantha muttered. Her gaze fluttered to Nate and then John. "Just a little...an—an accident."

John was sure those injuries were from anything but an accident. Had someone done that to her? Anger surged in him at the thought.

He'd seen firsthand the devastation that happened when people didn't treat others as humans. Alyssa had been a prime example, and his heart still broke at the memory.

"That must have been some accident," John muttered, soaking in her injuries.

Samantha shrugged. Her gaze fluttered wildly about the room, and she gripped her purse. "I'm sorry. I can't talk now."

"Can we help you get cleaned up, at least?" Nate asked. "I can grab my first-aid kit, put some ointment on that cut."

She shoved a hair behind her ear. "I'll be fine." She reached into her purse and pulled out a piece of paper. Her tremble was more noticeable when she extended her arm. "Here's the rest of my rent for the month. I'm afraid I'm going to have to take off. Family emergency."

"Anything I can do to help?" John asked, even though it wasn't his business to ask.

"No." She shook her head. "I'm just going to grab my things and pick up Connor. We're going to hit the road tonight."

Nate shifted, worry wrinkling the corners of his eyes. "You can't wait until morning?"

Samantha shook her head. "I'm sorry. But I've got to go now. This can't wait." She paused and sucked on her lip for a minute. "Look, you and Kylie have been really kind to me. I don't know how to say this, but please be careful. Be safe. Especially safe."

"What's going on, Samantha? I don't like the sound of that." Nate, a seasoned Coastie, had always been tough, strong and fair. Right now, he sounded on edge.

John wanted to step in, to say more, to help in some way. But he didn't know the woman, and Nate did. He held his tongue, restrained himself from pushing Samantha for answers. It was obvious that she needed help, even if she wouldn't admit it or accept it when offered.

She took a step toward the staircase leading to her apartment over the restaurant. "I don't have any time right now. I've got to go."

She rushed up the stairs. Halfway up, she dropped her purse and the contents clattered down. John retrieved some lipstick and a pen. He handed the items to her, noticing how she jerked back when their hands touched.

"Thank you," she muttered before hurrying away.

John stomped back down the stairs and joined Nate at the back door. He wanted to get his friend's take on the situation. They moved away from the staircase so their voices wouldn't carry.

"What was that about?" John asked.

Nate rubbed his jaw, looking just as perplexed as John was. "I have no idea. She's scared."

"Someone roughed her up," John muttered.

Images of Alyssa flooded his mind. He blanched at each memory before regret filled him. He should have done more to protect her. He should have known that the man who'd caused her so much misery in her past would return, that he wouldn't be content to leave her alone.

"I've seen that look before. She's terrified." John shook his head, unable to get the images to leave his mind. "What do you know about her?"

Nate shook his head. "Not much. She keeps to herself. Always pays her rent on time. Dotes over her son. But she's offered very little in terms of personal information. We don't ask. If she wants us to know, we figure she'll tell us."

John clenched his jaw, still replaying the conversation with her. "She said, 'Be safe.' It sounds as if trouble might be coming."

"I'll keep my eyes open. We've had problems around here before."

"And they landed you in the hospital," John reminded him. "Maybe I should stick around, be an extra set of eyes...."

"You do your thing, John. Smuggler's Cove is your dream. I'll take care of things here or call the police if I have to."

John hated to walk away when a storm could be brewing. Especially since Nate and Kylie had a toddler and another baby on the way. Nate would need all the help he could get.

John prided himself on always being there for friends when they need him. That's one of the reasons why his failure with Alyssa hurt so much.

He'd let her down. He'd let their unborn baby down.

"I don't like this," John finally said.

Nate clamped his hand on John's shoulder. "It's about time you did something for yourself. The change of scenery will be good for you."

But John didn't know if he could do that. The image of Samantha standing in the doorway with fear in her eyes would haunt him. So would the remembrance of her busted lip and the cut on her forehead.

Could he really go on with this new chapter of his life just as he'd planned? He didn't know.

Samantha's thoughts raced a mile a minute as she zipped her suitcase. Her jaw and her head ached. Even her eyes hurt as tears threatened to push out.

She had to get a grip. She had to pick up Connor and keep moving. And she didn't have much time.

Samantha didn't know where she'd go, how she'd get there or what she'd do once she arrived. All she knew was that she had to leave.

She gave one last glance at the apartment. At one time, she'd thought the small space was perfect. She'd wondered if they might find a home here in Yorktown. And maybe one day Kylie and Nate could be her friends.

She should have known better. A stable life—feeling normal and without fear—none of those things were her reality right now. The notion of a safe, happy life was only a farce.

Stepping back onto the landing, Samantha closed the door behind her. She heard the lock click, the sound cementing her plans to run.

Here I go...again. Lord, watch over me. Show me where to go. Pour Your wisdom over me.

Hauling her suitcases behind her, she thumped down the stairs. Her heart raced, pounding in her ears. Each pulse seemed to echo the urgency of the situation.

Go. Move. Run.

All she wanted was to find a place to stay. Rest. Be.

At the landing by the back door, she looked back. Just as she expected, Nate was standing there, waiting for her.

She'd known he wouldn't accept her flimsy explanation. His friend was gone, though. *John* was gone.

That was probably good. The man's eyes had seemed too intense, too curious...too compassionate. She feared her reaction to him. Whenever he'd come into the restaurant and Samantha had spotted him, her heart had raced.

The man was attractive. Really attractive. He was tall with dark, neat hair. His body looked sculpted and firm. He seemed to be a loyal friend to Nate and Kylie. He wasn't the loud or pushy type. Instead, he seemed steady, patient and strong.

"Samantha, are you sure you have to go?" Nate asked. Concern stained his eyes, pulling her back to reality.

She nodded, her throat dry. She crept closer and closer to the door, unable to stay in one place. "I'm sorry. I hope I didn't bring trouble your way."

"Trouble?"

She licked her lips, panic fluttering through her. "I've said too much already."

What was she thinking? She should have just slipped away quietly. Too bad there wasn't a training course for how to effectively go on the run and disappear off everyone's radar. The problem was that Nate and Kylie had a toddler, and a baby on the way. She'd never intended to put them in harm's path.

"Maybe Kylie and I can help...."

"No one can help, but thank you." She stared at him another moment, wishing she could offer more of an explanation. "Thank you for everything."

He finally lowered his chin, his lips pulled into a tight line. "Be safe."

She nodded again. "Thanks."

She stepped outside into the warm, dark summer night.

She really had liked it here. Living above the little restaurant. Enjoying the waterfront, the shops, the history.

The area had seemed so safe, so quaint and friendly.

Her desire to keep her son safe trumped her wish for a stable life, though.

She ambled across the parking lot, pulling her suitcase and heaving Connor's backpack up higher on her shoulder. Was she really ready to start another new life? Exhaustion pulled at her at the thought.

As she rounded the corner, a figure in the shadows caught her eyes.

Oh, no! He was back. The man from the grocery store.

Samantha wasn't sure she had enough fight left in her to survive another confrontation.

TWO

Samantha broke into a run, not bothering to look behind her. She had to move quickly. Had to think fast. Had to be smart.

"Samantha, it's me."

The voice sounded familiar. She slowed her steps but only for a minute. After all, Billy's voice had been familiar. Familiar didn't mean safe.

"It's John, Nate's friend. I didn't mean to scare you."

She slowed again. Hesitated. Finally, she turned. Her entire body was tense, ready to flee if necessary.

John raised his hands and stepped toward her. Maybe he hadn't been in the shadows, as she'd first thought. His truck door was open, as if he'd just climbed out. Maybe he'd spotted her leaving before he'd pulled out of the parking lot.

"I saw you leaving," John confirmed. "I wasn't trying to hide or frighten you."

"What do you want?" She didn't care if he was Nate's friend. She didn't know who she could trust right now.

He stuffed his hands into the pockets of his jeans. "Look, I don't know what's going on. I didn't even plan on doing this. But I won't be able to live with myself if I don't say something. I have a feeling there's really not a family emergency."

"It depends on how you define family emergency." Her family—she and Connor—were definitely in the middle of an emergency situation. The thugs hired by Billy had found her. And if they caught her, they'd kill her. They wouldn't bat an eyelash before taking her life. She wouldn't be so lucky to get away again the second time around.

He pulled out a piece of paper. "If you're looking for a place to get away—and a job—here's an idea for you. It's not much, but you'd have a place to stay. A safe place."

She glanced down at the card, tempted by the offer. She didn't have any other plans. No ideas even. "Smuggler's Cove? I've heard of the island before. One of my friends in high school lived there for a while."

"It's one of the safest places I've ever been. Everyone knows everybody. The biggest crime is littering. I'm fixing up some cabins there. I could use a hand painting, restoring some furniture, making the structures livable."

She stared at him. His words sounded sincere. But she couldn't shake her general distrust of people. "Why do you want to help me?" After all, didn't everybody want something? Nothing was free or sacred. Not even marriage, apparently. She'd learned that the hard way.

John shifted. A new heaviness seemed to press down on his shoulders. "I've been in some tough spots before. I get what that's like, and I hate to see people struggle."

She held her head up higher, struck by the sincerity of his words. But she couldn't let herself soften. Being weak would get her killed. "Thanks for your kindness, but I've got to go."

He looked away and shoved a hand in his pocket. "Right. Family emergency."

She nodded, unsure why she felt the urge to pour everything out to him. What would it be like to let someone else help carry her burden? It was an idea she couldn't let herself consider because the crushing reality was that she was all alone. Now and forever. "That's right. Thanks again."

Before he could say anything else, she climbed into her car and took off to pick up Connor.

The next morning, John stared at the beachfront cabins in front of him. His thoughts should be on the task before him—the major, he'd-bitten-off-more-than-he-could-chew task. The task that could easily turn into a money pit.

Instead, he was still thinking about Samantha Rogers. He couldn't help but wonder if she was okay. Or try to figure out where she'd gone and why she was so scared.

He wanted to help. But they didn't have that kind of relationship. They didn't have any kind of relationship, for that matter. To even say they were acquaintances would be stretching it.

The woman was an adult, he reminded himself. She could ask for help if she needed it. He couldn't make Samantha trust him. She had no reason to.

Which was why he simply needed to dig into his work and concentrate on his own issues. The good Lord knew John had enough problems of his own that he shouldn't try to take on anyone else's, as well.

But something about the look in her eyes reminded him so much of Alyssa. Helping Samantha would in no way atone for the failings of his past, he reminded himself. But something still drew him toward the situation. Something brought out a protectiveness in him and made him want to intercede.

He put those thoughts aside and continued making a list of everything that needed to be done. Before John had arrived, he'd had a plumber and electrician come out. With those tasks done, he could work on the rest of the restoration process.

There were eight smaller cabins surrounding one larger one in the center. They'd been fishing cabins twenty years ago until the owner had died. The owner's son had no interest in staying on the island, so the structures had been abandoned until two months ago when the son had finally put them on the market.

Smuggler's Cove was one of John's favorite haunts when he was out boating and fishing. The island had great seafood and a quiet pace of life that fascinated him. He'd known he needed a life change. When he saw the cabins, he knew what that change should be.

His plan was to fix them up and rent them out to fishermen, vacationers and people who just needed some time away. He certainly knew what it was like to yearn for a place where time had slowed. He knew the healing powers of being on the water. John realized that sometimes only time and reflection could heal broken, grief-stricken hearts.

He circled one of the cabins, compiling a list of all the supplies he needed. The bulleted list had already filled one page. Now he was starting on his second. At this rate his savings wouldn't last long.

At least he'd still have the comfort of the summer breeze. The scent of the bay seemed to soothe him, along with the squawking of seagulls, the sound of crashing waves, the heavy, salty air.

As he rounded the corner of one of the cabins he spotted a woman and child approaching in a golf cart. Alvin— the town's "chauffeur," as he called himself—was at the wheel. John stopped and watched as Alvin unloaded two suitcases, waved hello, and then sped off to his next job. No doubt there were other tourists waiting to sightsee on the island. This was prime tourist season; the time when businesses counted on making enough money to sustain them all year.

The woman and boy grabbed their luggage and started across the sandy path toward him.

His heart quickened as he recognized the woman. "Samantha."

She'd tried to cover up the cuts and bruises with makeup but it hadn't worked. Still, the woman was striking.

She raised her chin. "I hope that job offer is still available. I've reconsidered and I'd like to work for you."

"I can arrange that." His heart lifted. He still didn't know why he felt so protective of a woman he hardly knew, but he had to believe that God had brought Samantha and her son here for a reason. Their meeting last night was no coincidence.

"Great." She looked beyond him, wincing when her gaze reached the cabins. "Those are yours?"

He glanced behind him and frowned. The task did seem overwhelming, maybe even foolish. "These are going to be my life for the next couple of months."

"Big job." Her gaze still fixed on the houses in the distance.

"You up for it?" He watched her expression. When her eyes met his, John saw curiosity there.

She nodded slowly, surely. "Definitely."

"The cabins aren't much, but a couple are in better shape than the others. Pay is free rent, plus $100 a week. It's not much, but it should get you groceries and cover any other expenses."

"Sounds fine."

John nodded behind her. "Who's this with you?"

Her arm went around the boy's shoulders. "This is my son, Connor."

"Nice to meet you, Connor." He guessed the boy to be around eight. He was the spitting image of his mother with blond hair, big eyes and milky skin.

The boy squinted against the sun and frowned. "Nice to meet you, too." He sounded less than enthusiastic.

"I thought I should let you know that I have worked construction before," Samantha continued. She raised her chin, stubborn determination written all over the action. "I can do any labor that's needed."

"I'll hold you to that."

"Thank you. I'll work hard. I'm not looking for a hand-out."

"Understood." He liked it when people worked for what they wanted instead of accepting everything for free. He could respect that.

Just then, someone appeared from the gravel road that led to the secluded cabins, and called out a loud, "Hey!"

Samantha jumped, reminding him that she was in some sort of trouble, the details of which were unknown to him.

Samantha turned, and stared at the uniformed man in front of her, her heart pounding so hard that it felt visible, as if her entire body was pulsating with it. When she spotted the brown law-enforcement uniform her pulse only quickened more.

Time and time again, the police had let her down. She'd thought they were there to protect and serve. Instead, she'd found they were best at judging and condemning.

That much had been obvious when she'd been framed for a crime she hadn't committed. She should have stayed around to fight for her good name and reputation, but she'd seen the way justice wasn't always served, and she wanted no part of it. So she'd taken things into her own hands and fled with her son.

Now she lived in fear of being discovered.

"Can I go look at the water, Mom?" Connor's voice pulled her out of her thoughts.

Samantha looked down at her son and nodded. "Just don't wander too far away."

Just as Connor sprinted toward the bay, John turned toward her. "Samantha, this is Zachary Davis. He's the sheriff here on Smuggler's Cove."

She felt her face go pale as she nodded hello. Great. Her new boss was chummy with the local sheriff.

That meant her time on the island may not last as long as she might like. She knew she should have gone to a big city. But somehow she'd ended up here, on this remote little island where no one had cars, a place only accessible by boat.

As she'd thought about John's offer last night, she'd tried to talk herself out of it. But then she'd realized that Billy would expect her to run far. Staying close might throw him off her trail.

After she'd picked up Connor, she'd called a friend from work who'd agreed to meet her at a local park. Samantha had decided to leave her SUV there. It was obvious that someone knew her car's make and license plate number. She had to put distance between herself and the vehicle.

Lisa, a single woman in her mid-twenties, had taken her to a hotel. The next morning, Samantha had called a taxi.

"Where to?" the driver had asked.

Samantha had remembered the dwindling money in her purse. Using her debit card or credit card would be too risky. Billy could track her. He obviously knew her alias now. But the ferry to get to Smuggler's Cove was pricey. What if John had changed his mind once she'd arrived?

So much was depending on this one decision to come

here. Mainly, the lives of her and her son—and her son's life was the most important thing of all.

"What's going on, Sheriff?" John's voice pulled Samantha out of her thoughts.

The sheriff put his hands on his hips. "We've had some vandalism around here lately. I'm just trying to let the townsfolk know. I have suspicions that whoever is behind these crimes might have used these cabins as a hideout at some point or another."

"I'm sorry to hear that. I didn't think stuff like that happened out here." John squinted against the sun, which flooded his face. He had a five o'clock shadow that made him look rugged. His white T-shirt and worn jeans seemed to fit his persona better than the uniform Samantha had seen him wear in the past.

"It usually doesn't. But nowhere is immune to crime, not in today's world." The sheriff shifted.

He was youngish—probably in his late twenties, just like Samantha. He had sandy brown hair and blue eyes. Samantha noticed he didn't have the same island accent as the people down at the docks did.

"When did you get here?" the sheriff asked John.

"Just this morning."

"Take the ferry in?"

John nodded toward a boat bobbing in the water by the pier. "No, I came over on my boat. I figured I'd need it, especially if I had to go back to the mainland for supplies. The ferry's schedule isn't always mine."

"Well, it will be nice to have you around here. I might be able to use some of your expertise from your coast guard days, especially if these vandalisms continue."

"Anytime. But only if you show me some of those fishing holes you've been telling me about."

Samantha tuned out their conversation for a moment.

The sheriff's words caused Samantha to shudder. *Vandalisms?* Here on Smuggler's Cove? There wasn't anywhere one could get away from the bad in the world, was there? She wasn't naive enough to think there might be; she'd only hoped this place might be different. Might be safer.

At a lull in the conversation, the sheriff turned toward her. "You here visiting from out of town? I don't think we've met yet."

Her throat burned as she nodded. "I'm Samantha. I'm going to be helping to restore the cabins here."

"These places might need a bit of a woman's touch." He grinned personally. "Where you from?"

Familiar tension began pulling at her. Why did people always have to ask for details? "Everywhere actually. But I was raised in Georgia."

He tipped his head. "Well, nice to meet you, Samantha. Hope you enjoy your stay here. Make sure that John shares some of his fish with you. Nothing better than grilling out with the fresh catch of the day on the menu."

Tempting, but there would be no enjoying her stay. No, the only part of life she'd taken delight in over the past year had been Connor. He was her happiness. The rest of life... it scared the breath out of her.

As the sheriff walked away, John turned toward her. "How about if I show you to a cabin?"

Samantha nodded and called Connor over. Putting some space between herself and the rest of this town sounded perfect at the moment. Even if that meant hiding out in a shabby, drafty cabin that hadn't been used in years.

She knew the better end of a bargain when she saw one.

John unlocked the door to the cabin next to his. Of all the cabins, this one's structure was the most stable. It had electricity and plumbing. The furniture was decent.

The whole place still needed to be spruced up and aired out, but he figured it was the most sufficient for Samantha and Connor.

He pushed the door open and squirmed at what he saw inside. The whole place felt musty and dark. There were rust stains on the kitchen sink. A door hung slightly askew. The wallpaper peeled in the corners.

Maybe this wasn't suitable for Samantha. For anyone.

She seemed to read his thoughts. "This will be fine."

"It's not much." John looked down at Connor and saw the boy frown. He also saw Samantha squeezing her son's shoulder, probably a nonverbal message for him to stay quiet. Honestly, John wouldn't blame the boy if he had reservations about staying here.

"It just needs to be cleaned up a little," Samantha said as she examined the room with her gaze. "Needs a little paint, everything needs to be wiped down, maybe add some curtains and get rid of those dusty ones. It will be great."

The cabins weren't large—only eight hundred square feet or so. The front was a great room with a living room on the left, a dining room and kitchen on the right. The two spaces were separated by a breakfast bar.

A short hallway stretched beyond that. There were two bedrooms and one bathroom.

At least the refrigerator and stove worked in this cabin.

He'd offer them his own cabin, one that was larger. Except it wasn't in any better shape than this one. In fact, one of the bedrooms had a hole in the floor that he needed to patch. Way too dangerous for Connor.

"I'm thinking we should start here today," John said.

"Good idea." A smile tugged at her lips.

"I'll bring the supplies over, if you don't mind painting and getting a little dirty. You can start now. We'll get this place in shape for you."

"Not at all."

He stomped across the rickety porch and walked toward his cabin, where he kept his supplies. He couldn't believe that Samantha had actually come. If he'd even had an inkling, he would have started preparing this place earlier.

He'd followed his gut when he'd invited her here. Now his brain had to kick into action so he could figure out his next step. He needed to make a list of things she could do around here. Having her here was the right thing; he felt sure of it. But there were details that needed to be considered.

He grabbed what he needed and started back toward Samantha. As he approached the cabin, the sand soft—and silent—beneath his feet, he paused. A conversation drifted out from the open window.

"This isn't a discussion, Connor," Samantha said, her voice firm.

"I'm tired of moving, Mom. Why couldn't we just stay where we were? I liked my school. I liked my friends."

"It's not an option, Connor."

"But, Mom…"

"There's nothing to discuss."

"There's nothing to do here. This place is boring. There aren't even any cars. Probably no TVs. Not in here, at least. I bet you there aren't any kids my age, either."

"You might be surprised. And getting away from those video games will be good for you. Besides, you can help me work. Then you won't be bored." Her voice lilted near the end.

"This stinks."

"We're going to make the best of it. That's what we do. It's a good life lesson. A hard one. But a good one. We don't choose our circumstances, but we choose our attitude."

John had heard enough—enough that he felt as though

he was intruding. He knocked on the door, more curious than ever as to what their story was. He knew he couldn't ask.

Samantha pulled the door open and stared up at him with eyes as wide as full moons. "Mr. Wagner."

"Please, call me John." He held up his supplies, quickly observing that Samantha had already changed into some old shorts, a T-shirt, and had tied a purple bandana around her hair. "Let's get this place into shape. There's a washer and dryer at my place. You should probably wash the sheets and comforter. I bought them used from someone in town."

"I can definitely handle today's assignment. Especially since Connor will be helping me. Right, Connor?" She looked back at her son.

The boy frowned as he looked up from a handheld video game, his expression like most eight-year-old boys probably would have in this situation. Just then, John's phone rang. He saw Nate's number.

"Excuse me a moment." He stepped outside and hit Talk. "What's going on, man? You miss me already?"

"Ha. Yeah, I wish my reasons for calling were that simple."

That didn't sound good. "What's going on?" John focused on some seagulls fighting over something on the shoreline.

"I just thought you should know that someone broke into the restaurant last night."

"What?" Was this related to Samantha? It had to be. He didn't like the sound of this already.

"Yeah, someone went through our former tenant's apartment."

"Trying to find Samantha," John filled in the blank.

"Exactly. I think she's in trouble. Big trouble."

He remembered her sweet face, battered and bruised.

He thought about her little boy. "I hate to hear that. Any reason you wanted to call and tell me, though?" He hadn't mentioned his offer to Nate.

"We had to call in a police report. We gave the cops a copy of the rental agreement we had with Samantha, and they did a routine check on her driver's license number. It turns out there's no record of any Samantha Rogers, not one with her license number or at her previous address. She doesn't exist."

"What?" Was Samantha using an alias? Why? Just what was her story?

"The plot thickens, bro. There's more. After the local police came by, an FBI agent paid us a visit."

John's mind raced. What in the world was going on?

"He claims that Samantha isn't in trouble. He says that Samantha *is* trouble."

"That's ridiculous." Samantha was obviously scared, but nothing about the woman screamed devious.

"That's what he said. He said something about her being a suspect in the murder of her estranged husband back in Texas."

THREE

"A murder suspect? I don't believe it." John glanced across the sandy yard just as Samantha stepped onto the porch with an armful of sheets. Connor ran ahead of her, and she began racing after him. Connor giggled as his lead widened. That was not an image of a killer. Samantha, if anything, was a victim. "What did you tell him?"

"I told him I couldn't believe Samantha could ever hurt another person and that I had no idea where she went. It's the truth. I don't want to know. My guess is that this agent is trying to track her down, though. I don't know how long it's going to take."

"I don't think you ever answered my original question. Why are you telling me this?" John asked.

"Samantha texted Kylie last night and did an informal character check on you. She wanted to find out if you were a classy kind of guy."

"And Kylie said?"

"She said she'd trust you with her life. I know your past. I figured you might have passed on your contact information to Samantha. I just thought I'd let you know what happened last night. Just in case. I have a hard time believing Samantha's dangerous. But, should you see her, keep that in mind."

John did see her. She paused at his cabin doorway, then turned around to get his approval before going inside. When he nodded, she flashed a smile and then ducked into the doorway.

A killer?

Never.

But whatever was going on in her life sure had created a tangled web. If he were smart, he'd stay away.

But the chivalrous side of him couldn't stand to see a woman or child in danger.

He wasn't sure what he'd been thinking when he'd agreed to hire her. He knew what Alyssa would tell him. She would say that his heart was too big for its own good. Then she'd smile and tell him that's why she loved him so much.

There wasn't a day that went by that he didn't miss that woman. Time had made his grief more bearable, but it hadn't lessened his loss.

That's why he had to help Samantha while still keeping her at a distance. His moral duty was to aid someone in need. But helping was as far as it went.

After working a seven hour day, Samantha relished the tepid shower water. She was even thankful for the lousy water pressure as she scrubbed the grime off nearly every visible surface of skin. She had to admit that the physical labor today had felt good, despite her sore ribs and the tender skin around her eye.

She'd been working a desk job for the past few months. While working this new job, she found it invigorating to submerge herself into a task at hand, even better because Connor could work alongside her. Her injuries were grim reminders that not everything was as idyllic as it seemed here, though.

She climbed out, toweled dry, and pulled on some clean clothes. Then she rubbed the steam from the mirror and stared at her reflection. She noted the lines around her eyes and on her forehead. Those hadn't been there a year ago. The events of the past twelve months had taken a toll on every part of her—physically, emotionally and spiritually.

Her mom had once told Samantha that she was a survivor. She held on to her mom's proclamation, hoping it was true. But she didn't feel like one. Sure, maybe she'd managed to stay alive. But somehow, she hadn't felt as if she was truly *living* in a long time. Fear and guilt could be a prison of their own.

"You ready, Mom?"

She looked over at Connor, her heart squeezing with both love and guilt. "Sure thing." She dried her hands and then hooked an arm around her son's neck. "Thanks for helping today. Admit it—you had fun."

He shrugged. "I don't know if I'd say that."

The place had shaped up quickly. Samantha had washed everything, scrubbed the floors and peeled down wallpaper. It didn't look that bad after all.

Meanwhile, John had patched the roof, fixed a broken stair on the porch and removed a hornet's nest from outside. Connor had even gotten into the action. He'd helped with painting and had scrubbed the fridge.

They'd all worked together—in silence. Samantha was thankful. Talking led to questions, and she didn't want the questions to lead to lies.

"We're going to be okay, Connor," she assured him.

"Mom?"

"Yes?"

"I changed my mind. Can we stay here for a while? Please? I'm so tired of moving."

Her heart squeezed. "I think we can stay awhile."

"You *think?* That means you're not promising anything." Not much got past her son, and she wouldn't lie to him.

"It's complicated, Connor."

He frowned.

Samantha leaned down in front of him until they were eye to eye. "I'm doing the best I can. I hope we can stay here for a while, Connor. I really do."

"Promise me."

"I promise that I'll do my best to stay here. I know it's not exactly what you want to hear. But it's the most I can give you."

"Okay." He frowned again and reluctantly began walking with Samantha toward John's house. She should have refused John's invitation to dinner. But she had no groceries and no time to buy anything. Besides, having dinner with someone wasn't a promise of anything—not a promise of friendship or trust or anything other than a professional relationship.

Despite that, Samantha should have probably said no. Her jaw ached. She was tired. And she was scared.

The fewer people who saw her face here, the better. It was bad enough that the sheriff had already seen her. The last thing she needed was for him to run some kind of background check on her.

If he did, then she'd be out of a job, behind bars and Connor would have no one. The cops back in Texas still thought she was involved in the scheme her husband and his friends had devised. When Billy—the ringleader—had heard she was going to turn them in, he'd put money into her personal bank account—large sums of money. Money that made her look guilty. He'd planted emails that made it look as though she was the mastermind behind his scheme to scam people out of their investments. He'd lined everything up just right so that, if he fell, then she'd fall with him.

That's why it was so important that she remained low-key and not arouse anyone's suspicions.

The problem was that she could already see in her boss's eyes that he was perceptive and intelligent. How long would it take for John to put it together that she was running from both the bad guys *and* from the law?

If he discovered that information, would he turn her in?

The smell of a charcoal grill billowed in the air as they approached. John looked up from an old, park-style grill—one that was cemented into the ground—and grinned.

"How's the cabin coming?" he asked.

"I think it will be fine. I really appreciate your letting us stay here."

"I appreciate the help. I was sincere when I said I needed a hand."

Samantha paused by the grill, second-guessing herself for a moment. Maybe she should have refused his offer. She'd done such a good job keeping to herself. She couldn't let herself feel too safe here on the island. "Is there anything I can do to help get dinner ready?"

"It's nothing fancy. I'm fine. You can just relax."

Relax? She almost wanted to snort. She couldn't remember the last time she'd relaxed. No, she was always on guard, always alert.

Despite that, she sat in an old deck chair on the porch of John's cabin. Connor plopped on the steps and began running a stick over the sand, drawing pictures.

She looked out in the distance.

The Chesapeake Bay was blue and pristine. The sun was setting across the water, smearing pink and purple lights together. Wisps of dune grass sprinkled the area. Pelicans flew overhead, and the smell of seawater brought an unusual sense of comfort.

A false sense of comfort and security, for that matter.

"So, tell us about Smuggler's Cove," Samantha urged.

"It's a national treasure, if you ask me." John flipped the fish and a scrumptious scent filled the air.

Samantha took a moment to soak him in.

The man was gorgeous with his broad frame, his head full of dark hair, and his warm brown eyes. No one could deny that.

But that didn't matter to Samantha. It was the single life for her, from now until eternity. Every man she'd ever trusted had ultimately let her down. She didn't see that changing…well, ever. Men were all the same, as far as she was concerned.

At five, her father had left. Her boyfriend in college had cheated on her. Her husband had swindled people out of thousands of dollars, choosing money over his family.

She'd never met a man she could trust.

Which was why she needed to concentrate on something else at the moment.

"I think the neighborhood where I grew up is bigger than this place," she said, careful to not reveal too much about herself.

But her words were true. The whole island could only be maybe fifty acres. It was small enough that Samantha, as she'd traveled from the wharf to John's yesterday, had seen tombstones in people's front yards.

He chuckled. "You could be right. I think there's only around a thousand residents here. It's unlike any place I've ever been. At high tide, the waters rise and small wooden bridges connect various parts of the island. Only about sixty percent is inhabitable. The rest is marshland."

"I hate to see what that means during hurricane season."

"They say the island was formed from a hurricane and another one could easily erase it. In fact, there's an island north of here—locals call it the Uppards—that was once inhabited. Residents abandoned it about forty years ago because of flooding. The entire island became submerged during storms."

"It was probably a good idea that they ditched the place then." She crossed her legs, soaking in the sun for a moment. "What about the accent I heard on some of the locals. I wasn't imagining that, was I?"

John closed the grill and leaned against a picnic table. "Not at all. When the island was first settled by the British back in the 1880s—yes, we're talking nearly as far back as John Smith and Pocahontas—they were isolated. Really isolated. More so than they are now. Their way of life was preserved for a long time, even the accent stuck around. In recent years, it's become not as prominent with television and visitors and so."

"Fascinating. I didn't get a good look at what's here. I take it there's not a Macy's."

He chuckled. "No, no Macy's. But there is a general store, three restaurants, a bed and breakfast, the docks and the homes of the residents living here."

"Why's it called Smuggler's Cove?" Connor asked.

"Many years ago, pirates were said to have buried their loot on the island, thus the name Smuggler's Cove."

"So, if I look hard enough, I could find treasure? Awesome! Can I start now?"

Samantha shrugged. "Go for it. Just don't wander too far away."

As Connor scurried off, John turned toward her. "So, you said you had experience in construction?"

She nodded. "I worked for a construction company, doing their books. I also helped Connor's father with flipping houses. My uncle was a handyman, so he taught me a lot." Even her uncle had ended up leaving his wife for another woman. He'd totally lost contact with the rest of the family when that happened.

She leaned back into the chair, imaging herself living a different life. A life where she could sit back and relax and enjoy the world around her. But there was no need to dwell on what wasn't. She had to concentrate on survival. "How about you? Is this what you do for a living? Restoring cabins?"

"Nah, I quit my regular job at the Coast Guard Training Center. Decided I needed a change of pace."

Why would someone do that? Samantha wondered. But the question wasn't hers to ask. Not now. Besides, too many personal questions could be dangerous. She needed to stay on neutral ground.

She nodded. "Where are you from?"

"Texas originally. Gloucester for the past several years. Smuggler's Cove now."

Tension crept up her spine at the mention of Texas. "Really? What part of Texas?"

"The Houston area."

Just a coincidence, she told herself. He probably hadn't heard of Billy. Probably hadn't heard about what happened to her husband. But what if somehow he made the connection that her former husband was a part of the gang that had cheated the city's richest out of their money? What if he put two and two together?

She stared out to sea. The island seemed so secluded, so far off the beaten path.

But that seclusion would either keep her safe or keep her trapped.

"I just remembered a phone call I need to make," Samantha blurted. She had to excuse herself before her face gave way any more of her thoughts.

"Go right ahead. I'll finish cooking these fish. Dinner will be ready in no time."

She stood and plodded through the sand, going far enough away that John wouldn't be able to hear any of her conversation.

She walked toward the shoreline, noting how Connor dug holes in the sand not far away. Still searching for buried treasure. She smiled sadly as she looked over at him.

Reaching into her pocket, she pulled out a cheap track phone she'd bought from the gas station beside the hotel last night. She'd needed to call a few people, but she didn't want to be traced. She'd thrown her old phone into a river, trying to take every precaution possible not to be tracked.

She wished she could simply walk away from her life in Yorktown and disappear. But her boss was counting on her. He might call the police if she simply left without a word. And Connor's summer school teacher would worry if he just stopped going to classes. It was best she covered her tracks and made everyone think this was a last-minute trip. That way no one would call the police. The last thing she needed was a missing-persons report.

She cleared her throat and dialed her boss's number. A moment later, Hank came on the line. "Samantha, where are you?"

"I'm sorry, Hank. Something's come up. A family emergency."

"Man, Samantha, I'm sorry to hear that. Talk about awful timing, all the way around."

She bristled. "What do you mean?"

"You heard about Lisa, right?"

Samantha's muscles constricted. Lisa had promised not to say a word about their meeting. And Samantha hadn't even told Lisa where she was going. The fewer people who knew, the better. She'd only asked Lisa for a ride because she couldn't risk keeping her car. The thug who'd attacked her had seen the vehicle. He knew her license plate.

"No, I didn't hear." Her throat burned with the words.

"She died last night. She ran off the side of the road, apparently. No one really knows what happened. Rumor has it that she had some drugs in her system."

"Lisa didn't do drugs," Samantha said. "You know that."

And Lisa hadn't been high when she'd helped Samantha. An inkling of the truth began to creep into her mind. Someone had killed her and covered their tracks. Just like someone had killed Anthony and made Samantha look guilty.

"She's gone. I can't believe it. And now you're not here. I don't know what I'll do without you two ladies."

"I'm sorry, Hank. I really am."

"Come back as soon as you can, you hear?"

"You got it."

As she hung up, cold, stark fear swept over her.

Lisa… Not Lisa. This was Samantha's fault. She'd put her friend in danger. She should have been more careful, tried to be more independent.

Now her friend was dead.

Guilt pounded at her conscience. If she could only go back, she'd do things differently. She'd keep her friend out of this.

But it was too late to change anything of that.

She'd managed to escape these thugs before. Why did she feel as if her time had run out? All of the running in the world wouldn't make her feel safe right now.

FOUR

John noticed the change in Samantha when she returned from her phone call. He wondered what kind of conversation she'd had. He hadn't missed the pallor that had come over her at the mention of Texas, either.

He kept reminding himself to mind his own business. But minding his own business wouldn't help keep anyone safe.

Just then, Lulu appeared down the sandy walkway leading to the cabins, a large dog pulling her along.

His dog.

Rusty was a rowdy Australian Shepherd he'd found wandering outside his house three months ago. The dog hadn't gone away, so eventually John had adopted him. Now it followed him everywhere, perhaps as his eternal way of saying thanks.

John liked to grumble about the dog, but he had to admit that Rusty had become a faithful companion. Lulu was the island's local groomer, and John had dropped Rusty off with her this morning after she'd promised a free first visit.

"Hello, there!" Lulu called. Lulu was a heavyset woman with orange hair and too much makeup. But she was a friendly soul.

Rusty broke free from the leash and stampeded over

to jump on John. The dog's tail wagged and he continued to jump, sixty-five pounds of hyper joy. John grabbed the leash before the dog greeted Samantha and Connor with an equal amount of enthusiasm.

"A dog!" Connor exclaimed.

Connor giggled in delight when Rusty began licking his face. A moment later, Connor and Rusty took off running down the shoreline together. John thanked Lulu, who looked exhausted, and then turned back to Samantha.

"You've just made a friend," Samantha mumbled. "Connor has wanted a dog forever."

"Rusty's been wanting a little boy to call his person for a long time, too, so they should get along just fine."

John finished cooking, and when Connor came to join them, something nearly impossible happened. Rusty followed him and stayed at Connor's feet. The canine didn't run off or even look longingly down the shoreline in search of seagulls or other critters.

Traitor.

They all sat down at a weathered picnic table in front of John's cabin. He'd thrown an old sheet over the benches, hoping no one would get a splinter. Funny how he hadn't given that a second thought up until a few hours ago.

"What's there to do around here?" Connor asked, taking a bite of his burger. John had cooked a couple, just in case Connor didn't like flounder.

John looked at the water. "Go to the beach, fish, crab."

"That sounds boring. Well, maybe not the beach. Not if I have a boogie board. Do you have a boogie board I could borrow?"

"I might be able to scrounge one up for you. But have you ever tried fishing?" John took a sip of his soda, amused by the boy's expressive face.

He shook his head.

"Well, I'll show you sometime." Great, he was making promises. That was something he'd vowed not to do. He didn't want anyone depending on him, especially not Samantha.

"Can I put the worm on the hook?" The boy's eyes were wide with excitement.

John glanced at Samantha. A halfway amused expression feathered across her face.

"Do you *want* to put the worm on the hook?" John asked.

Connor nodded, mustard from his burger slathered across his top lip. He didn't seem to notice—or care. "I do."

"Then definitely."

"What else is there to do?"

John looked off in the distance again. Those weren't questions he'd thought about. He'd only been focused on his cabins. "Some boys in town like to play kickball. You ever played?"

"No, I just do karate."

"Well, maybe you can teach them some karate, and they'll invite you to their kickball games. How does that sound?"

He shrugged. "Okay, I guess."

John looked over at Samantha to see how she was taking their conversation. At the moment, she appeared distracted. Her gaze constantly scanned the area around them. Any of the earlier amusement was gone.

He stared at that bruise on her jaw. John had a feeling it wasn't from an accident—a fall or car crash or walking into a wall. He also noticed her hand reaching for the side of her rib cage when she thought no one was looking. The woman had been beaten up. The thought caused anger to surge in him.

Samantha must have noticed him staring because her hand went to her jaw.

Connor jumped in. "She fell in the grocery store parking lot."

A rigid, quick smile fluttered over her face. "I'm kind of clumsy."

"Why do I have a feeling there's more to the story?" he asked.

Her face tensed. "Nothing more, and nothing that you should concern yourself about."

He didn't question her, even though curiosity burned inside. Everything about the woman was mysterious…and slightly suspicious.

The rest of the conversation revolved around what needed to be done on the cabins, where to get groceries, and what to expect during tourist season.

When everyone finished eating, Samantha started to help him clean up, but the sound of a boat puttering in the distance interrupted them. He looked up to see a Bayrunner creeping up to his pier, a man waving from the bow.

He approached the man, noting how Samantha stayed back. Still, he could feel her wide eyes on him, watching everything that happened.

"You the owner of this place?" the man on the boat asked. The man appeared to be in his mid-forties and had the look of someone who spent a lot of time in the sun. His skin was so tanned that the wrinkles around his eyes remained paler than the rest of his face. He had longish blond hair, that was swept away from his face.

John nodded. "I am."

"I'm Kent Adams, a real estate agent from Richmond. I've been trying to find you for the past month." The sunset blurred behind him.

"Why would you want to find me?" John placed his hands to his hips, his guard going up.

"I have a buyer who's interested in your land. He's willing to pay handsomely for this piece of property. He said it's perfect for his retirement home."

"But this land isn't for sale."

"We were hoping we could change your mind. We're talking an amount where you wouldn't ever have to worry about money again. You could quit your day job, find another nice little plot of land, and enjoy yourself."

"I'm not interested. Thanks for the offer." He started to walk away when the man called him back. John paused.

"Take my card in case you change your mind." The man extended his hand, a piece of cardstock at the end. "Maybe talk to your pretty wife about it first." He nodded behind him at Samantha.

"There's nothing to talk about."

"At least hold on to this, just in case."

Against his better instincts, John backtracked and took the man's business card. He didn't plan on using it. No, the cabins were his. He had plans for them—plans that didn't include becoming rich, but becoming whole and healed.

Samantha's gaze looked fragile when he returned. Her arms were crossed, her eyes focused on the boat puttering away in the distance. Meanwhile, Connor was talking to Rusty who had nothing but attention for the boy.

"Everything okay?" she asked.

John shoved the card in his pocket. "Someone inquiring about the land."

"Is that odd?"

Her *question* was odd, but he didn't mention that. "Maybe a little. It's like Murphy's Law, though, isn't it? This property has been abandoned for years with no interest. As soon as I snatch it up, someone else decides they want it."

"Life is funny sometimes." She nodded back to her cabin. "I should get going. I need to get rested up for a full day of work tomorrow."

"Anything you need from me?"

She shook her head. "No, we'll manage with what we've got."

With that, she called Connor over and started back to her cabin.

Just what was that woman's story?

He probably shouldn't dig too deeply, he reasoned.

She needed help, and he had agreed to give it to her.

But still, curiosity burned inside him.

Samantha couldn't sleep. She couldn't stop thinking about the fact that Lisa had died. Guilt continued to pound at her, and she mourned for her friend.

How had she died? What had happened in the moments leading up to her death? Had she suffered? Her thoughts then turned to Lisa's family, to worry about Connor, to anxiety about everything else in life.

Her only comfort was in the fact that she was here now.

This place was no Hilton. But at least it was a place to sleep. A place to feel safe, if just for a night.

There was no telling how long they'd be here. Best-case scenario: through the summer. Worst-case: mere days.

She'd be on guard. She'd keep an eye on the sheriff, on John. If anyone seemed to recognize her, if anyone asked too many questions, she'd catch the next ferry. If that didn't work, she'd borrow John's boat. It was docked on the pier outside the cabins. How hard could it be to operate the watercraft?

Finally, realizing the futility of sleep, she threw the

covers back, stood and went over to the living room window. Against her better instincts—in spite of her fears of someone breaking in—she'd cracked it open before turning in for the evening. Without AC, the place was hot. It would be unbearable to try to sleep in the stuffy cabin with the humid, ninety-degree weather. A nice breeze floated over the bay, but the only way to appreciate it was to open a window.

As she stared outside, she wondered if she should have gone somewhere bigger, somewhere she'd blend in. But the island seemed so secluded, like such a peaceful hiding spot. She hoped she didn't regret the decision.

Then she thought about the man on the boat who'd paid John a visit earlier. Could he have been hired by Billy? Had he come out searching for her under the ruse of trying to buy property?

She didn't know. Maybe she was reading too much into it.

But those men had gotten to Lisa. Poor Lisa. She'd been such a sweet friend. She'd had no idea about Samantha's past. She'd had no idea where Samantha was going. She'd been innocent.

Despite that, they'd killed her.

That just went to prove that Billy and his cronies were ruthless. They were hot on Samantha's trail and didn't want her to get away again.

Not just that, they wanted to kill her. And if they did, Billy and his henchmen would flaunt it to everyone they could. They would make an example of her, showing what happens to people who betray them.

Killing her estranged husband hadn't been enough. They also wanted her blood.

Anthony had left her three months before she'd discovered the scheme he and his friends had developed. The two of them had had endless fights over his work hours, his increasingly erratic behavior and the influence of his friends. Financially, they were better off than ever. But their relationship had otherwise gone downhill.

He'd left her and filed for divorce. Then one day, Anthony had shown up at the front door, sweat across his brow, demanding to pick up something he'd left in their home office. Samantha had refused to let him come inside. She'd feared that he might fly into a rage, and she didn't want Connor to see his father like that.

She'd finally closed the door, and Anthony had left.

Then she'd been curious.

What had he wanted so badly? His visit had motivated her to go through the items he'd left at the house. After searching the desk once more, and in a moment of dumb luck, she'd discovered a false bottom in one of the drawers. Inside were his company's books. She'd glanced at the pages, and what she'd seen had blown her away. Her husband had been scamming people.

She crunched the numbers and compared the figures to other records left at the house. That was when she'd realized that her husband and his friends had been embezzling from some of the city's wealthiest. They'd promised a twenty-five percent return on their investments for flipping houses. Instead, her husband and his friends had kept all the profit for themselves.

She confronted Anthony, and he denied her accusations. Then he'd gotten quiet and asked her not to pursue her theories any further. He'd warned her that asking questions could lead to trouble.

Samantha hadn't listened. She'd thought it was just an empty threat. She'd told him he had two days to come clean himself or she was turning the books over to authorities. Anthony had begged her not to.

Never had she imagined that in those two days, one of his friends would come up with a way to frame her. Nor had she imagined that her husband would be killed in a car crash. And she *never* would have imagined that Billy, Anthony's best friend—and a cop—would frame her for Anthony's murder. He was the mastermind behind everything, the one calling the shots.

The police had brought Samantha in for questioning, and it became clear she was going to take the fall for Anthony's murder and the supposed part she'd played in the investment scheme. When she'd been let go on bail she'd grabbed the telltale books and fled.

It hadn't been the smartest thing to do. But Samantha had done it.

Now, here she was today. She'd hidden all the evidence she'd taken with her in a safety deposit box. The law—including Billy, under the guise of doing his job—was chasing her. If Billy found her, she'd pay the ultimate price for her betrayal.

He wouldn't get her. The fighting instinct in her knew she wouldn't let that happen. She'd defend herself—and her son—with every last breath. She'd gotten this far.

Samantha had been on the run for the past year. Every time there was a hint that Billy or one of his hired men might be close, she'd fled. It hadn't been an easy life, but it was better to keep moving than chance being killed. Better than it would have been if she'd stayed and been convicted of a crime she hadn't committed. Then Connor would have no one. Samantha's dad was long gone. Her mom was in and out of rehab—in other words, unreliable.

The other men involved just did Billy's dirty work. Samantha had suspicions he was blackmailing them. That was the way he operated—by manipulation. The man who'd attacked her last night had been a stranger, no doubt someone who'd been hired.

Billy was serious. He was scary. And he was determined to find Samantha.

It was too bad the police wouldn't help. No, the police couldn't be trusted. Billy and his friends had planted that money in Samantha's bank account—somehow and someway. Samantha still wasn't sure about the details. She hadn't stuck around long enough to find out. To go online now and snoop around was risky. She didn't want to do anything to lead the police to her door.

The breeze fanned her face. She closed her eyes for a moment and let herself think about what it would be like to be carefree. To be on this island on vacation. To be able to relax and enjoy herself and have fun without always having to look over her shoulder.

When she opened her eyes, she realized they were moist. No little girl ever imagined at the beginning of her happily-ever-after story that things would go this horribly wrong. Her life had become a living nightmare.

She stared at the moon over the bay. It was bright and luminous. It sent a trail of light over the water.

Samantha glanced over at John's cabin. The man seemed nice enough. And he kept to himself. That was a good thing. Keeping distance from people was almost a requirement right now. It often left her feeling empty, but at least Connor would remain safe. That was all she could ask.

At least Connor had made a new best friend in Rusty by being here. Good. The dog would distract him and keep him occupied. John didn't seem to mind.

She smiled when she thought about Connor squealing with delight as Rusty chased him along the shore. That boy had always wanted a dog. But she could never get him one.

What would happen if they had to pick up and leave? A dog would only get in the way.

She hoped he didn't become too attached.

A noise in the distance caught her ear.

She tensed. What was that? It almost sounded like a scratch.

She needed to find something—anything—to protect herself with. She glanced around and realized she had nothing in the nearly barren cabin.

Creeping across the floor, she grabbed a bottle of body spray she'd left on the kitchen table. It wasn't much, but maybe she could douse the intruder's eyes and buy some time, if that was what it came down to.

She paused by her suitcase and listened again. There was that sound. Someone was walking across the porch, nestled close to the wall and just out of her vision.

If she put the window down, the intruder would hear her and know she was inside. But if she left it up, gaining access to the house would be too easy.

She hunkered against the wall.

She glanced across the way. Through the open door across the small hallway, she could see Connor asleep in his bed. He didn't have a clue what was going on. Good. That was the way she wanted it. For now, at least.

Another footfall sounded. And then a shadow covered the moon that had once flooded into her cabin.

She bit back a scream and prepared herself to fight.

FIVE

John startled from his sleep at the sound of Rusty's barking. What in the world was going on? Darkness stared at him from his windows. Nighttime had fallen several hours ago.

If Rusty was barking, something was wrong.

He threw his legs out of bed, pulled on a sweatshirt and shorts, and rushed to his front door. Rusty was there, his hair standing on end.

"What is it, Rusty?"

The dog barked even more feverishly, turning in quick, urgent circles.

As soon as John opened the door, Rusty jetted outside. He stepped around his porch in time to see a shadowy figure disappear into the trees behind the cabins.

What in the world? There *had* been someone out here. They'd come from the direction of his new employee's cabin.

Apprehension crept up his spine. He hoped and prayed Samantha and Connor were okay.

Taking long strides, he hurried toward their cabin. He rapped on the door, trying to tamp down his apprehension. Trying not to think about worst-case scenarios.

No one answered, and his urgency grew. He pounded on the door again. "Samantha. It's me. John."

The door flew open. Samantha stood there, her eyes as wide as sand dollars and anxiety wrought across her face. She appeared unharmed, though. He thanked God for that.

"Is everything okay?" His words sounded strained, even to his own ears.

She squeezed her sweatshirt at the throat and nodded. "I heard something. I thought…"

"Rusty heard something, too. He chased off whoever was here."

"Who…?" She shook her head.

Her fear looked too familiar, as if the emotions never left the depths of her soul. That was no way to live.

He shrugged. "I have no idea. I haven't had any trouble since I've been here. Maybe it was just someone curious about the work I'm doing on these cabins." He knew there was far more to it, but he didn't want to scare her. She was already scared enough.

"Right."

He stepped closer, hesitating, wanting both to pry and to keep his distance. "Is there anything I should know? If I had more details, maybe I could help."

Her whole body became rigid. "There's nothing to know."

"That's right. Those bruises are from an accident." He kept his voice light but firm. Maybe he shouldn't have said it, but the woman could hide a lot of things…but she couldn't hide those injuries. In the black and blue, the truth told its side of the story.

She touched her forehead. Rubbed it. Looked in the distance before looking back at John. "Look, it's like this. I don't want to lie to you, but I don't want to tell you the truth, either."

He wanted to reach out and touch her arm, but he restrained himself. "Someone hurt you."

She stared at him a moment, swallowing deeply. "Someone wants me dead. I just need a place to lie low for a while. I don't want to cause any trouble."

"Maybe I can help."

"I appreciate that, but the less you know the better."

He remembered what Nate had told him about the FBI agent who'd stopped by. Was there any truth in the man's accusation? Was that why Samantha couldn't tell him any details? Or did she truly just not trust anyone? "If you say so."

He took a step toward the door, realizing he wouldn't get anything else out of her. It was her choice, and he could do nothing about it.

"John…."

He paused and looked up. "Yes?"

Samantha's eyes brimmed with tears. "If anything happens to me, will you make sure Connor is okay? I just need to know that someone will watch out for him. I know you hardly know us, but maybe you could take him to Nate and Kylie." Her voice cracked.

His heart ached at the vulnerability of her words. "Samantha, if you let me help, I'll make sure nothing happens to you and Connor." He started to reach out, but his hand dropped to the side.

She pulled a hair behind her ear. "I wish I could believe that, but I can't afford to trust someone again. I can't be let down."

"What makes you think I'll let you down?" Images of Alyssa tried to squeeze into his thoughts. He pushed them back. Not now. Now wasn't the time to dwell on his past failures.

She pressed her lips together a moment. "Experience." Her voice didn't waver. She believed the words.

"Experience can either hold us back or act as a launching pad for change. At least, that's what *experience* has taught me." He shifted, not knowing what else to say. "I'll come by in the morning and put new locks on your place, just to make sure you're safe. I'll also move up replacing the windows here higher on my list. I'll get the kind with safety latches so you can still sleep with them open, but with a little more security and peace of mind. It can get pretty hot out here at night."

"I appreciate that." She still clutched the collar of her shirt as though her chest was tight. Her entire body looked tight for that matter, as if the wind gusted she might break.

"I'll leave Rusty outside tonight. If anyone comes back, he'll alert you." *And me, too,* John thought to himself. He wanted to know if there was trouble brewing.

Kylie and Nate had saved him when he was on the brink of losing his career, his friends, his faith. He wasn't going to let Samantha down. He needed to at least pay it forward.

"I can't thank you enough for your help."

He stooped down to see her better. "You going to be okay?"

She nodded, straightening slightly as if to cover up her fear. "Of course. I'll be fine. At least, Connor slept through all of this. That's a blessing."

"It is. We don't want him to freak out. Being cautious and on guard is good, though."

"Absolutely." She stared up at him, her eyes wide and as luminous as the moon outside.

He paused another moment. He didn't want to leave, and he wasn't even sure why. But his throat squeezed with pressure, and his feet seemed rooted where they were. Finally, he nodded. "Don't hesitate to find me, if you need anything."

"It's a deal."

He hated to walk away. But he reminded himself that Rusty would be out here. John doubted anyone would return. Not tonight, at least.

In the morning, he'd talk to the sheriff, see if he could patrol around here more often. In the meantime, he'd keep his eyes peeled.

He had a feeling he wouldn't get much sleep tonight.

No, he had too many things on his mind. One of those being Samantha Rogers.

The next morning, Samantha knocked on Connor's door and went inside. "Rise and shine, Sunshine."

Her son opened one sleepy eye. "Already?"

"That's right. We've got another long day." A long day following a long night, Samantha thought to herself.

He frowned. "You know what I miss about our old place?"

Her heart squeezed, a feeling that was all too familiar. "What?"

"My friends Owen and Mackenzie, and my karate classes."

She sat down on the edge of his bed. "I know changes are hard."

"At least I have Rusty here." He threw his covers off and started to get dressed.

Samantha shuddered as she walked back into the living room and remembered the events from last night. After John had left, she'd put all the windows down. The cabin had grown warm and humid, but she'd pulled the covers up to her chin anyway. She couldn't stand the thought of being an easy target. Mostly, she couldn't stand the thought of Connor being an easy target. Not on her watch.

She'd listened for any more telltale sounds that someone was here again. Once she'd heard the dog's nails tapping against the porch. She'd heard the wind scattering sand against the wooden planks of the exterior, and Connor's deep breathing from his room.

In her mind, she pictured Billy creeping around, waiting for the chance to strike. Then she remembered that Billy always had someone else do his dirty work. The person outside her cabin was essentially faceless.

But Billy couldn't have found her yet. No one knew where she was. She'd covered all of her bases. Then who had been on the porch?

The vandals the sheriff had talked about?

That was the only thing that made sense.

Or was that the only thing that she *wanted* to make sense?

Finally, she'd drifted off to sleep, only to be confronted by dreams of intruders, carjackers and fists colliding with her face.

Back in the present, Connor hopped out of his bedroom, trying in vain to put a shoe on while moving. Samantha remembered she had nothing for breakfast. She'd need to walk into town and get some groceries. She didn't know when John would pay her, so she'd have to stretch her cash out for at least a week.

"Let's take a walk," she told Connor, hoping that possibility might cheer him up.

He frowned as he pulled his shoe on, but at least he didn't argue.

It was bright and early as she and Connor stepped outside. Her watch confirmed that it wasn't even eight o'clock yet. Hopefully they could make it to the store and then get back in time to work.

She cast a glance at John's cabin. He was probably sleeping. He deserved to after that late-night interruption. The concern on his face yesterday had nearly broken her. It had been a long time since she'd had anyone concerned about her well-being. If she was honest, it felt nice to feel looked after.

Waves rolled onto the shore, seagulls circled the sky, and boats floated in the distance. Everything appeared normal with no indication of what had happened last night. It was funny how life worked that way sometimes.

As soon as they started down the path to the store, Rusty appeared beside them. Connor's face lit up. "Hey, Rusty boy. You going to come to the store with us?"

The dog panted happily and kept walking.

Samantha enjoyed hearing her son talk to the dog. At the moment, he seemed happy and satisfied. He deserved a little contentment in his life. Samantha hoped that he might find it here, that he wouldn't resent her for yet another move.

The morning sunlight already beat down on them, but a nice breeze off the water interrupted the heat wave. It's too bad she wasn't on this island for different reasons. She might actually enjoy it here.

Smuggler's Cove was so off the beaten path; it was like the place that time had left behind. The island was a novelty within itself. No cars. Everything seemed slower and more enjoyable.

They reached the end of the lane. A row of houses stretched in front of them and in the distance she could see the town. That was where the docks, the wharf and the six or seven shops that comprised the "town" area of Smuggler's Cove were located.

Around her, the island was coming to life. A woman rode past on a bicycle and called hello. The golf cart taxi she'd taken yesterday drove past, Alvin offering a wave. She could see people moving down at the docks, getting ready for another day of fishing and making tourists feel at home.

"Rusty's the best part about this place," Connor muttered, patting Rusty's head.

Samantha smiled. "You think? How about the beach?"

"I guess I could get used to it." He skipped backward, patting his legs so Rusty would follow.

"You used to always beg me to take you to the beach, you know. When you were a toddler, you loved it there."

"I loved it because Dad loved it. It's not the same now." His gait slowed. Samantha remembered how hard Connor had taken it when his father had died.

She wanted to take her son into her arms and tell him that everything would be okay. But he was eight now. He wasn't into public displays of affection. And she doubted anything she could tell him would make him feel better. She would try anyway.

"He'd be really proud of you, you know." She tried to honor her husband's memory. Her son deserved to think his father was amazing. Every boy should think of his father as a superhero. He had plenty of time to learn the truth when he was older.

He scuffed the ground with his foot. "Yeah."

"I mean it, Connor. Your father always loved you." Even if he had secretly been a criminal. The thought turned her stomach. Had Anthony known that Billy would plant evidence to implicate her? That he set it up so she would take the fall?

Her decision to run caused her stomach to clench every day. It may not have been the best thing to do, but in her haste to protect her son, instinct had kicked in. She couldn't protect Connor if she was in jail. Anthony's cronies could have gone after her son, for that matter. And considering Billy was a dirty cop, she had no faith in the justice system.

Officer Billy Walsh had been one of those overly friendly guys who could win people's trusts in a heartbeat. He was good-looking with golden hair, blue eyes, and a quick smile. He knew how to say just what people wanted to hear so that he could get what he wanted. Samantha only wished she'd seen through him sooner. Her husband had trusted him; *she'd* trusted him. The man was like poison, though. One of those wolves in sheep's clothing that the Bible talked about.

"Beautiful day," someone called behind her.

Her heart leapt all the way into her throat. She glanced behind her, her shoulders achy again, and saw a man with wire-framed glasses, a golf shirt and khaki pants.

Keep calm. Don't raise suspicions. She forced a smile instead. "It is beautiful out here."

He double-timed a couple of steps and caught up with her. The man appeared to be in his late twenties. From his pale skin, she'd guess he wasn't from the island. His gaze was way too curious for her comfort. "You must not be a local. I don't hear the accent."

She had no desire to share too much with this man. But she couldn't afford to be rude, either. She needed to keep a low profile. "No, I'm definitely not a local."

"Fascinating place, isn't it? This Smuggler's Cove has such a unique culture and people, a real gem."

She nodded, wishing she could think of a way to gracefully end this walk together. But she had to get to the store and back. She didn't have time for any detours. "Definitely. I guess you're not a local, either."

"No, I'm with a travel magazine. I'm staying for a couple of weeks so I can write an in-depth article on the island. Sounds cushy, huh? It's my first big assignment. I come from the financial world. I wrote for accounting publications for years. I'm finally getting to do my dream job."

"Good for you," she managed.

The store was just a few blocks away now. She desperately wanted to reach it and be done with this conversation. Perspiration had started to sprinkle across her forehead.

This whole walking everywhere thing was strange. At least in a car she had a certain measure of privacy. Here, everyone seemed to have time for a stroll and a chat.

"I'm Derek, by the way."

"I'm Sam," she responded. Connor and Rusty trotted gleefully ahead. It was better that way. She only hoped John didn't get mad that Rusty had come with them. It wasn't as if they'd invited the dog along. He'd just kind of followed.

"Samantha!" someone bellowed behind her.

She froze. Who would know her in Smuggler's Cove? And then she slowly turned.

SIX

It was John, Samantha realized. Just John.

He jogged toward her. Seeing him filled her with a certain amount of relief. She seemed to instantly trust the man. Things usually didn't end well when she trusted that easily.

She forced another smile and waved as she waited for him to catch up. He immediately extended his hand to Derek and introduced himself. Derek didn't seem the least bit ruffled by John's tall, broad form. He affably offered his hand and chatted.

John cast a glance at Samantha as Derek launched into his same speech, and she felt as if she could read John's thoughts. They seemed to scream, *What are you doing?*

Finally, Derek turned toward the docks. "I'm taking a tour of the Chesapeake Bay today. Should be a good day for a boat ride." He paused and waved. "Pleasure to meet you both."

They said goodbye and then stood there for a minute, staring after him as he walked away. When he was out of earshot, Samantha turned to John, a burning question on her mind.

"He's a travel writer yet you didn't tell him about your cabins. Why?" Samantha asked.

John shrugged nonchalantly. "He's a stranger. I don't trust strangers easily. Until I know who was snooping outside the cabins last night, I thought it would be best to keep some details to myself."

Samantha nodded, liking John more and more as time went on. "Sounds smart."

They continued walking toward town. The sand sprinkled across her tennis shoes. A bicyclist rode past and waved. Two teens carried a canoe over their heads, laughing at something.

"Where are you taking off to so early this morning?" John asked.

"I needed to pick up some supplies. We didn't discuss what time I was starting this morning, but I thought if I was back by nine, that would be okay. I needed some breakfast if I was going to be worth anything today."

"Most important meal of the day." He nodded ahead to where Rusty chased Connor playfully. "It looks as though their friendship is continuing to grow."

Samantha glanced at Connor as he ran in circles, Rusty chasing him. "Looks like a match made in heaven."

"I just wanted to let you know that we're going to work on your place today. We'll have your cabin in order so you can have more of a home there, with a fully functioning kitchen and everything."

"Thanks. That's very generous." She liked the idea of having a home. Something about it warmed her. She couldn't get attached to that idea, though. It would only make her weak.

His smile faded. "No more problems last night?"

She shook her head. "No. I do appreciate you checking on us, though."

"Any friend of Kylie's is a friend of mine."

Samantha shrugged and kept walking. "To say we were

friends would be stretching it. I did enjoy talking to her when I had to opportunity, though. She seems genuine."

"She is. Her husband and I have been best friends for years." Early morning sunlight hit him. He needed to shave, but the stubble across his cheeks and chin only made him look more rugged and manly. His features were solid, making him appear like a rock inside and out.

Anthony's eyes had always sparkled with new adventures and possibilities. He'd gone wherever the wind had tossed him, always thinking something better was just over the horizon. Samantha's mind returned to the present. John had said something about Nate and Kylie. "That's great that you're such good friends. It's just too bad you're so far from them now."

"Only a boat ride away. Besides, they're supposed to come over next week and check things out."

Samantha nodded. It would be good to see Kylie again. "When's your goal date to open the cabins?"

"I would love to be finished before August."

"That's a lot of work." The cabins were charming, but time had weathered the buildings. John had a real task ahead of him.

"I have another friend who might be coming out to help."

"A friend? That sounds nice." She wished she were just asking out of curiosity. Nearly everything in her life was done out of fear, though.

"I knew him from the coast guard. He got out early and is looking for some work. He also has a friend he's talking about bringing with him."

She pushed down her panic. Their arrival shouldn't scare her. Unfortunately, everything seemed to scare her lately.

She decided to change the subject to something safer. "You miss the training center yet? Life back in Yorktown?"

When his face darkened, she had second thoughts about asking. "It's hard to say," John started. "I have a lot of bad memories there. The change here is good."

John seemed, by all appearances, to have it all together. But there was something he was hiding, some hurt in his past. The nurturing side of Samantha wanted to dig in, to uncover his hurts and try to fix them. The pragmatic side of her cautioned that she should stay back.

They reached the store and John opened the door for her. As she squeezed past him to go inside, their arms brushed. Electricity buzzed through her.

Those words of caution echoed in her mind. *Stay back.*

She needed to listen to that rational side and keep her distance.

But it was going to be harder than it sounded.

The work this morning had gone by relatively quickly. The first thing John had done was replace Samantha's locks, just as he'd promised. He'd ordered some new windows for all the cabins. That hadn't been at the top of his priority list, but now he saw the importance of doing so. It would take a few days for them to come in, though.

He'd have to keep an eye on everything in the meantime.

Samantha had been a quiet worker. She'd scrubbed floors, helped clear some of the junk out of the houses and opened all the windows to air out the structures.

Connor had helped some. When he'd gotten bored, he'd run around and played with Rusty. He'd overheard Samantha telling him earlier that they could go to the beach this evening, if he behaved.

She approached him now, a smudge of dirt across her

face. A few tendrils of hair escaped from her ponytail. She had rubber gloves on her hands and smelled faintly of Pine-Sol.

And, for some reason, his pulse raced for a moment. He scolded himself for the reaction and tried to look casual as she got closer. The last thing he wanted to think about was a pretty woman.

Using the back of her hand, Samantha wiped some hair from her eyes as she stopped in front of him. "The floorboards are rotting in one of the cabins. And it looks as though there's a leak in the roof."

He paused from repairing the porch. "I thought that might be the case. I'll move on to that one next."

These cabins were going to be more work than he'd imagined. The only relief from it, and the hot summer sun, would be the nice breeze coming from the water. Like it was today. Still, he loved digging in and getting his hands dirty. He could do this.

Out of the corner of his eye, he spotted someone coming down the lane.

Sheriff Davis.

John stood and stretched, his muscles taut from hunching over the railing. Just as he waved hello, he saw Samantha take a step back.

"I'm going to... I'm going to keep working," she stuttered.

Her face had gone pale, her voice trembled, and her hands shook. He thought about the FBI agent who'd shown up at Nate and Kylie's place. Should he mention that visit to Samantha?

Before John could make a decision, she hurried back to the cabin from where she'd come.

Interesting. Why would she react like that? Certainly the woman wasn't some kind of fugitive. He didn't get those vibes from her. So why did she look so scared at the sheriff's approach?

"How's it going, John?" Davis stopped in front of him, his hands hooked on his belt.

"Not too bad—except for the fact that we had an intruder last night."

Sheriff Davis's eyes widened. "An intruder? Did you see his face?"

John shook his head. "Rusty chased him off. He was dressed in black, plus it was dark out here."

The sheriff nodded. "It's especially dark out here, away from everything. In case you haven't noticed."

"It's hard not to." The solitude and removal from the busyness of city life was one of the many reasons he loved it here.

"I'll keep my eyes open and ask around. If it happens again, call me."

"I appreciate that."

The sheriff's gaze traveled across the property to where Samantha pulled a kitchen table out from Cabin 3 and began sanding it down. "How's your new employee working out?"

John rubbed his chin before nodding. "Just fine."

"Know anything about her?"

John shifted, unsure why the sheriff was being so inquisitive. "My friends back home know her and trust her. That's enough for me."

"I just like to have a general idea about our long-term visitors."

That was just the opening John needed.

"Speaking of long-term visitors, have you met that reporter guy yet?" John pulled on his work gloves, knowing he needed to get busy soon.

"Sure. What's his name again? Derek?"

"That sounds right."

"I met him. Seems like a sincere guy. He's been interviewing people all over the island. Seems eager to impress his editor." The sheriff shifted. "Why? Something I should know?"

John shook his head and grabbed a hammer. "No, nothing. I guess I'm just as suspicious of strangers as the next person."

"I'll patrol past here more frequently, just in case someone comes back. If anything else happens, let me know."

John grabbed a box of nails, not ready to end this conversation. "Who on the island might be wanting to cause trouble?"

Sheriff Davis looked into the distance for a moment. "Of course we have a couple of guys who could be more responsible citizens. My guess is that whoever is behind this isn't from this island."

"Any idea why someone would come to these cabins?" John followed his gaze and saw two sailboats breezing by in the distance.

"Could be any number of things. Maybe they're used to them being deserted and used to squat here. Or maybe it's not about the cabins at all."

John glanced over at the cabin. Samantha brought a chair out and opened a can of paint. She was doing exactly what he'd asked her to do and being a model employee. A sense of mystery still surrounded her, though.

"I'll keep my eye on things." John looked away from Samantha, hoping she had nothing to do with any of this.

As Samantha continued to scrape old paint from the table of another cabin, she tried not to glance back at the sheriff, tried not to show her discomfort. Her awkwardness was probably hard to miss, though.

She shouldn't have scurried off like she did. Her guise of having a lot of work to get done was true, but her hasty departure might raise questions. She had to be more careful.

John and the sheriff glanced her way. She forced a smile and a wave. Why were they looking at her? Was the sheriff telling John about her past? Would Sheriff Davis charge over here and arrest her any moment now?

Anxiety gripped her until her breathing became labored. What should she do? Run?

But how would she get Connor in time? Plus, she needed her things. There was no way she'd get off this island without any cash to her name. She might as well be on Alcatraz Island.

Calm down, Samantha. Calm down. It's probably nothing. They're just shooting the breeze.

She continued to scrape, but her mind was anywhere but on the task at hand.

Finally, the sheriff took a step her way. Fight or flight kicked in. She wanted desperately to run, to get out of here. But she needed to think more clearly. Until she knew more, she had to act unruffled.

The sheriff nodded her way and kept walking, all the way to the lane leading into town. When he disappeared out of sight, she breathed a sigh of relief. She had to stay under the radar. She'd work, keep to herself, and keep Connor safe. That was her prayer, day after day.

But how long could she continue to live like this? She was tired. Worry and anxiety could do that to a person. The emotions could rob them of sleep and rest and peace.

Samantha often wondered if she should have stayed in Texas. If she should have pled her case. If she should have hoped for the best instead of assuming the worst.

If she wasn't a criminal before the charges against her

were raised, she was now. She'd run from the law—fled before they'd had a chance to find her guilty.

But she'd seen it in their eyes. The police already thought she was a criminal.

In one way, Billy's plan had worked. She'd fled before turning over the information that would get him locked up. On the other hand, Billy wouldn't stop until she was dead. Her dilemma came in that turning over the information would put her at risk. Most likely, they'd take her into custody first and ask questions later. She'd gotten herself into a real mess and there were no clear solutions.

She felt sure that coming here was a good idea. Certainly none of the locals were a part of the group of men after her. That would be too coincidental. But she'd keep her eyes open for strangers who may have followed her.

She'd keep her eye on the sheriff, too. Samantha would look for any indication that he'd checked into her background. At the first sign of trouble, she'd run. And she'd keep running for as long as she had to, doing whatever it took to keep her son safe.

By the time Samantha fell into bed that evening, she was bone tired. Connor wouldn't admit it, but he was, too. He'd fallen right asleep. It was probably a mix of the heat and running around all day. After she'd finished working, they'd gone to the beach and he'd bodyboarded and jumped over waves and searched for seashells.

She'd been well aware that John was in the background, watching them.

Not because he was up to no good. She sensed that he was on guard now, especially after the man had been outside her cabin last night.

She shivered just thinking about it.

Tonight, the windows were closed, but John had brought

over a box fan for her room and Connor's. She was grateful for the relief from the heat, but the volume of the fan would easily mask any telltale signs that someone was trying to get in.

It didn't matter how tired she was; she couldn't sleep. She had too much on her mind. Instead, she got up, quietly crossed the room and peeked in on Connor. He was sleeping soundly in his bed. She smiled as she watched his chest rise and fall.

He was the one who'd gotten the short end of the stick throughout all of this. He deserved better. But until she could figure out how to make that better happen, this life would have to do.

She stepped back into the hallway, and headed toward the kitchen to grab some water.

That's when movement caught her eye.

She froze.

It was dark out here, far darker than what she'd experienced in other places. Right now, the black inkiness stared at her, concealing any signs of trouble.

She searched for the source of her tension, probing the shadows for a signal that something was wrong.

Had she been seeing things?

Was the movement simply the breeze creeping in through the cracks of the window and causing the curtains to sway? Or could it be Rusty poking around on the porch?

Her gut told her no.

Her gaze shot to the kitchen counter. Was there a knife in here? A baseball bat? Anything?

Before she could take action, a figure stepped from behind the couch.

She gasped.

She *had* seen something.

Even worse, someone!

The man wore all black, including a mask across his face. She could only see the gleam of light hitting his exposed eyes. He was looking right at her, and his gaze wasn't friendly. It looked downright menacing.

The man didn't say a word. But in two seconds flat, he'd crossed the small cabin and lunged at her.

She ducked, desperate to get away. She took off for the front door, hoping to lure the man out of the house and away from Connor.

But the man grabbed her arm and swung her around. Her head hit the door frame and stars swam in front of her eyes.

She reached for something—anything—so she could keep her balance. She had to think clearly; she had to protect her son.

The man's fist collided with her cheek. The force of the impact left her sprawled on the floor. She tried to pull herself back up, but the man kicked her. Pain surged through her rib cage.

Who was this man? Why wasn't he saying anything? Was he going to kill her, right here and right now?

Against her will, a whimper escaped.

She rose to her knees, tried to crawl away.

The man grabbed her hair and yanked her up.

When she saw his eyes, she knew she was going to die.

She lifted up a prayer for Connor.

Lord, please keep him safe. Please!

SEVEN

John lay in bed. He couldn't sleep. Instead, he reviewed all he knew about Samantha. Was the FBI agent right? Had troubled followed her here? He just couldn't pinpoint what kind of trouble someone like Samantha might be mixed up in. As much as he told himself it wasn't his business, he thought about it anyway.

A noise in the distance caught his ear. It was a crash, and not from an ocean wave breaking on shore.

He sat up in bed, his heart quickening. Had the intruder come back again tonight?

He threw on his clothes and dashed from his cabin.

Another crash shattered the usual serenity of the beach. It sounded as though it was coming from…inside Samantha's cabin?

His jog turned into a sprint.

He didn't bother with niceties when he arrived; he threw the door open.

Outrage filled him when he saw a man holding Samantha by the throat.

Before he could reach them, the man dropped Samantha. She crumpled to the floor like a rag doll. Then the intruder took off toward the back of the cabin.

John rushed toward Samantha, bending down beside

her. Blood trickled from her forehead and lips. "Are you okay?"

She nodded, but he saw the tears rushing down her cheeks. Recognized the pain flashing in her eyes. Felt the fear in her trembling bones.

She pointed in the direction the man came. "Go," she whispered. "I'll be fine."

He prayed Samantha was well enough to be right about this. Then he took off after the man. He'd gone out the window in Samantha's bedroom.

John climbed out after him. His feet hit the sand with a thud. He searched the landscape around him, looking for an indication as to where the man had gone. A moment later, he spotted him on his pier.

He sprinted after him, but the man was so far ahead, there was little hope John could catch him. That wouldn't stop him from trying, though.

The intruder jumped into a boat. Five seconds later, he had the engine cranked and sped away.

John stopped at the end of the wooden planks. His gaze was fastened on the boat, trying to remember any detail. But it was so dark outside he barely made out the make or model. Two men were on board, though, and both were wearing black.

Finally, when the boat disappeared, he jogged back inside to check on Samantha and Connor.

Speaking of which…where was Rusty? Why hadn't his dog alerted him that something was wrong? That in itself sent up a red flag. Rusty was an excellent guard.

He'd check on the dog later.

He stepped into Samantha's cabin. She'd pulled herself up to sitting and rested against the refrigerator. Blood trickled from her temple and her lips. Her eye was already bruised and swollen. The way her arms wrapped around her midsection, she was in pain.

"Where's Connor?" he asked again.

The fact that the boy wasn't out here alarmed him. He'd only seen one person fleeing the cabin, though.

Samantha rubbed the skin between her eyes. "He can sleep through anything. He's in his bed still."

Relief flooded him. He squatted beside her, trying to figure out the best approach. He knew she was a strong woman. Would she reject his help? He had to try. "You're pretty banged up. I should call the doctor, maybe even take you back to the mainland to the E.R."

She closed her eyes. "No. I'm fine. Really. Just a little sore."

"Are you sure you don't have any broken bones?"

She pulled her eyes open. They looked dull and defeated. "Pretty sure."

He desperately wanted to do something. "How about I help you to the couch?"

She nodded again. He took her elbow and gently prodded her to her feet. From the way her face scrunched with pain, the man had done some damage. Anger rushed through his veins, but he pushed the emotion down. "Are you sure you don't want me to call the doctor?"

"I'll be fine. I just need some pain reliever and maybe some ice. A bandage or two. It's nothing that won't heal." Her face told a different story. It showed just how beat up she was.

He wanted to wrap an arm around her waist, but he feared hurting her ribs. Based on the way her arm was slung across her midsection, she'd probably been kicked there.

He really wished she'd see a doctor, but he couldn't

force her to. In fact, he had a feeling that pushing would only cause more resistance.

Finally, he lowered Samantha onto the couch. Her head drooped against the back, and she shut her eyes. "Will you check on Connor for me? Just to be sure he's okay?"

"Of course." John crept down the hall, nudged the boy's door open, and heard the peaceful sound of his heavy breathing.

Samantha was right—the boy could obviously sleep through anything. The thought was both comforting and disconcerting.

He closed the door again—not all the way, but enough that any more noise would be blocked. He had to talk to Samantha and find out what was going on.

He only hoped she'd actually share more information with him.

John lowered himself beside Samantha on the couch.

"Connor's fine," he started.

"Thank goodness."

He knew he had to tread carefully. He barely knew the woman, yet his concern for her made her seem familiar. The adrenaline that charged through the room heightened everything, complicating an already complicated situation. "Do you have any Tylenol or a first-aid kit?"

She shook her head. "Not yet. I don't suppose the store's open at this hour, is it?" She attempted to laugh but it fell short.

"I can run get mine. You going to be okay here by yourself for a minute?"

She nodded, but her whole body seemed to tense at the prospect. He hated to leave her. But she needed to be cleaned up.

"I'll be right back." His mind raced as he hurried back

to his cabin. Who would do something like this? Why would someone attack an innocent person?

He wasn't naive. He'd seen his share of atrocities while in the coast guard. He knew evil existed. But seeing Samantha hurt like this sparked a new kind of outrage in him.

She was a single mother. Alone in a new place. She had no possessions to steal. She hadn't been here long enough to make anyone mad. So why?

He'd have to figure it out later. He quickly grabbed his first-aid kit and hurried back to her. When he walked in, he saw that she was still curled up on the couch. Her eyes were open now—probably watching for a sign that the man had returned. Her gaze softened when she spotted John.

"He left. On a boat. We're okay right now." He sat down beside her and pulled out the ointment. He squirted some on a piece of gauze and patted the cut on her temple. "Any idea who that man was?"

"Not a clue," she whispered.

"Did he say anything?"

She flinched when the ointment hit her skin near her lips. "No. That was the strange thing. He didn't say a single word."

He paused and stared at Samantha a moment. She really was beautiful. Her face had such clean, smooth lines. Her skin was unblemished, her hair glossy, styled neatly even now. "Samantha, I really think we need to call the sheriff."

"No!" She paused and shook her head. "I mean, I'm okay. It's no big deal." Her voice sounded softer, but rough edges still crept from her tone.

He tried not to sound pushy, but he needed to make his point. "He needs to know what happened, Samantha."

She squeezed her lips together and moisture filled her eyes. "What will it matter? The man is long gone."

"He might have killed you if I hadn't gotten here when

I did." He hated to remind her of the horrid facts, but he had to get through to her.

She visibly shuddered. "But he didn't. Now he knows I'm here. He won't come back. I was probably in the wrong place at the wrong time."

He studied her face. She tried to hold her chin up, tried to look certain. But her voice trembled. Her eyes looked too downcast. "You don't really believe that, do you?"

She said nothing.

He put a hand on her knee, trying to ground her. "What's going on, Samantha? Maybe I can help."

"No one can help," she whispered. "Especially not the police. Please don't mention this. Please!"

As soon as John left, Samantha sprang to her feet— at least, she sprang as much as her ribs would allow her. She had to get out of here. She should have known better. Should have gone someplace bigger. Someplace where it was easier to disappear.

There was no time to reflect on that now. Now, she had to get her things together. She'd sneak away before John knew she was leaving. After all, the less people who knew anything, the better. If she told John, he might ask questions. It was better if she simply vanished.

Her only regret in all of this was Connor. She hated to do this to him, to uproot him again. But his physical safety was the most important thing. She could deal with the emotional fallout later. She dreaded it, but she had no other choice.

She threw all of her clothes into her suitcase and glanced at her watch.

It was four-thirty. The ferry didn't leave until nine. She had to leave now, though. Maybe she could charter a boat.

Only that would take up most of her money. She really needed to conserve her cash.

Despite all of this craziness, she had to give Connor the best life possible. She didn't want to end up living in a car or, even worse, on the streets. She had to make sure her son had food to eat and sufficient clothing and a general sense of safety.

Tears sprang to her eyes and she sank to the floor. She rested her pounding head against the wall.

She didn't want to admit it, but she was tired and scared.

She was so tired of running.

So tired of always being afraid.

Of always looking over her shoulder.

Of always fearing the worst.

This was no way to live. Yet what other choice did she have?

She couldn't just go to the police. They would arrest her. Then what would happen to Connor?

Lord, I'm at my wit's end. I just don't know what to do anymore. I don't know how to make things better. I don't know how to protect Connor. I just don't know anything.

It wasn't only her body that ached; it was her soul, as well. How much more could she take before she broke? Before the damage became irreparable?

Finally, she wiped away her tears. She had to stop feeling sorry for herself. That would only make her weak; she had to be strong if she wanted to survive.

She'd finish packing up her things, wake Connor, and they'd wait at the docks. Maybe a nice local would volunteer to take them across the water. There were other options, not just the ferry. She just had to be smart.

Samantha glanced around the cabin. It was too bad things here hadn't worked out. If circumstances were different, this island might have proven to be lovely. She'd always dreamed of living in a place that had a slower pace of life. She dragged herself into the bathroom and flinched at her reflection in the mirror. She definitely had to clean herself up before anyone saw her. One look at her cuts and bruises and they'd run far away.

To the best of her ability, she used her makeup to hide her battle wounds. She pulled on a hat, hoping the bill would shadow her bruises. Then she got dressed. Her ribs ached, but she pushed past the pain. Finally, she went into Connor's room and shook him awake.

His sleepy eyes looked up at her. "What's wrong?"

She wiped his hair from his face and put on a brave face. "We need to get going."

He jetted upright, his gaze darting to the window. "Going where? It's still dark outside."

"We need to leave." She grimaced, hating the fact that she had to do this.

"Again? I don't want to leave again." Stubborn determination crossed his face.

She swallowed, her throat achy. "We have to, baby."

"But I like it here!"

Her heart squeezed. "I do, too. But it's not safe here anymore."

"But—"

"No arguing, okay? Let's get you dressed and get your things packed."

He pouted, showing his unhappiness. Samantha didn't approve of his pouting, but she couldn't fuss at him, either. She didn't want to leave, so she knew exactly how he was feeling.

She glanced at her watch again. It was already five-thirty. Soon, the sun would be rising. She had to hurry.

* * *

John couldn't get Samantha out of his mind. He wished he was only thinking about her smile. Instead, he was thinking about her bruises, about her cuts, about her secrets.

He leaned against his porch, staring at the reflection of the moon over the water. The crashing of the waves usually comforted his heart when little else could. But not right now.

Rusty lay panting at his feet. He'd found the dog locked in one of the cabins and, based on the remainder of a bone, someone had given him a steak laced with something to knock him out.

That meant that whoever had come tonight had planned their visit. They'd known about Rusty. They'd known where Samantha was. He'd probably been the same person who'd come the night before.

Even more disturbing was the fact that Samantha had panicked at the possibility of involving anyone else in this, including doctors or the police. Just what was going on?

She hadn't asked him for help, so John should keep his distance. Yet, he knew he couldn't do that. He couldn't take a backseat in this, not when the woman seemed to have no one else.

He glanced at his watch. It was almost five-thirty. He knew his friend Nate always rose at four-thirty to get things ready at the restaurant. He'd be awake.

On a whim, he dialed his friend's cell phone. Before the first ring completed, Nate answered. "John?"

"Did I wake you?" Guilt pinged through him. Nate had one small child and another one on the way. Sleep was a commodity hard to come by. He hoped he hadn't called him on the one morning he was sleeping in.

"No, I'm prepping the kitchen. What's going on?"

"I have a question for you. It's about Samantha. Did the police ever come back? Did they figure out who broke in?"

"No, they didn't. The FBI agent came back, though. Asked if we'd heard from Samantha yet."

"And you said...?"

"I told him the truth. We haven't heard from her."

Some of the strain across John's back disappeared. "She's here, Nate. I offered her a job helping me restore these cabins."

"I had a feeling you might have."

"Someone broke into her cabin and beat her up last night, Nate."

"Man, really?" Surprise laced Nate's voice. "That's some scary stuff."

He saw movement by Samantha's house and stiffened. "Listen, I need to run. Can you have Kylie call me when she has a chance?"

"Of course."

John hung up. He started to hurry across the sand, but then he thought better of it. What if the man had come back? He didn't want to announce that he was there. He needed to be more subtle.

He swung around to the back of his cabin. The darkness worked in his favor right now, concealing him. He braced himself for another fight. This time, the man wouldn't get away.

The sand padded his steps. But what he heard stopped him in his tracks.

Whispering.

Two people whispering.

He squinted as he peered around the side of the cabin and he braced himself for a confrontation.

EIGHT

There were two figures. Silhouettes, really.

And they were pulling something behind them.

He stepped closer.

Suitcases?

That's when he realized who the intruders were.

Samantha and Connor.

And they were trying to leave.

Alarm rushed through him.

Even though he kept telling himself this was none of his business, it still felt as if it was. He barely even knew the mother and son. But somehow, he felt that he had to protect them, to help them in some way.

Was it because he remembered seeing the same look in Alyssa's eyes that he saw in Samantha's? The same fear?

He hadn't been able to help Alyssa. He'd tried. He'd really tried. But her abusive ex-boyfriend had found her. In a mad rage, the man had set their house on fire. John had arrived home from his business trip early—but not early enough.

Just as he'd pulled onto their street, the whole place had gone up in flames. He'd tried to rescue her, even had a scar across his chest to prove it.

He didn't want to scare Samantha and Connor, so he

cleared his throat before stepping out from the shadows. "Hey, guys. What's going on?"

Samantha gasped and nearly jumped out of her skin. Her shoulders relaxed some as he stepped more fully into the moonlight. "John? Is that you?"

"I was on the porch when I heard something. I wanted to make sure…" He glanced at Connor. He wasn't sure how much the boy knew. "I wanted to make sure everything was okay."

She tucked a hair behind her ear with one hand and her grip intensified on her suitcase with the other. The woman was wound tighter than a snake about to strike.

"It's fine."

He nodded toward the suitcases beside her. "You going somewhere?"

"Mom says we have to leave again," Connor muttered with a frown.

"Connor!" Samantha cautioned.

The boy shrugged and pulled his backpack up higher.

It was time that John asked some of the hard questions he'd tried to keep inside. He kept his voice even tempered. "Samantha, could I talk with you for a minute?"

He saw the hesitation on her face. He knew she was going to say no and to keep walking, keep running. Instead, she surprised him with a nod. "Okay."

"Connor, you want to watch cartoons in my living room?"

"You have a TV?" The boy's eyes lit up.

"Sure do." John smiled. "If it's okay with your mom, you can go see what's on."

He looked up at his mom. "Can I?"

Samantha nodded. "Of course. Just don't make a mess."

"I have some donuts from Erma's, also. She makes them homemade. Help yourself."

As the boy took off toward his cabin John and Samantha stood there, awkwardness shifting between them.

"Do you mind if we sit on the porch?" Samantha asked. "I want to be close to Connor. Just in case—" she shrugged "—you know."

He knew. Just in case the thug who'd broken into her cabin came back. "Sure thing." He grabbed the suitcases and carried them to his porch. Samantha settled into a rocking chair there.

"How about some coffee?" he started.

"I'd love some, if you don't mind."

"Not at all." He already had a pot percolating. He poured two mugs, grabbed a couple of donuts and took them outside. He half expected that Samantha might take off the minute he took his eyes off her. But not without Connor, he realized. He could tell that boy was her heartbeat, her reason for living.

He let silence pass for a minute until finally he started. "Running's not the answer."

She raised her chin, staring into the distance stoically. "What makes you think I'm running?"

"That's what it looks like to me."

She continued to stare at the bay, quiet for a moment. He let her have space to sort out her thoughts, to make decisions about how much to say. He hoped that space would work in his favor, that she'd trust him.

"Say I was running…why would that be a bad idea?"

"Your problems always have a way of catching up with you." He shifted to face her better. "Samantha, maybe I can help. I know you don't know me that well, but I can't stand to see a woman scared. Or a child, for that matter."

"That's noble and kind. I appreciate the gesture, but, if I can be frank, why should I trust you?" Her tentative gaze met his.

"Have I given you any reason not to?"

She stared at him another moment. When she opened her mouth, he fully expected her to deny anything was wrong, to feign more excuses, to shut him off.

He braced himself and tried to plan his next move.

Knowing he couldn't help unless he was aware of the whole story.

Finding out the truth could very well put him in trouble with the law. He'd known he didn't want to go back to his old job at the Coast Guard Training Center. But this information could very well cement that decision, leaving him nothing to fall back on if this new business venture failed.

It was a chance he was willing to take, though.

"Look, you risked your life for me, John," Samantha started. She hated the uncertainty in her voice. But it was real. There were so few times she let any genuine emotion show. "You didn't have to do that. You don't have to do any of this. In fact, it's better if you didn't, probably. I don't want to pull you into anything."

Now, why had she said that? She hadn't spoken of what had happened with anyone since she'd fled. Why was she opening up to this virtual stranger? Was it because there was something in his eyes that beckoned her trust?

"I can handle myself, Samantha. Don't worry about my safety. It's you that I'm worried about. You and Connor. You think if you keep running that whoever is after you won't catch up eventually. I've learned sometimes it's better to stand your ground and prepare yourself for battle rather than to run."

"It's really complicated, John." She had no hope he would understand. Not many people had been in her shoes. She wasn't even sure why she was here. Why she hadn't run. Was it Connor's pleading? John's sincerity? Ignorant hope?

"Maybe I can help make it uncomplicated." He put his coffee on the porch railing and leaned forward.

"I don't think anyone can help with that."

"Listen, when I was young, my father was abusive toward my mother. She always moved me from place to place. Probably every six months, we went somewhere new. My mom was afraid my dad would find us, I guess. I didn't realize that until I was older. When I was younger, I couldn't stand how much we had to move. I couldn't stand the lack of stability in my life. I resented my mother for it. At the time, I didn't understand. Now I do. Now I know that she was doing what she thought was best."

"What happened with your mother?" Samantha asked.

"Eventually, my real dad got cancer and died a few years later. My mom, in the meantime, met a great man. They married when I was nine. I still think of Walter as my dad."

Samantha smiled, the action bringing with it bittersweet emotions. She hoped that Connor would have a father figure in his life one day. He was fine at this age. For the most part, at least. But once he hit the teen years, he was going to need someone to help him navigate life. She could help to an extent, but not like a father could.

"Connor's dad is dead," she finally offered. After John had opened up as he had, maybe she could trust him with a few details from her past. "He was in a car accident."

"I'm sorry to hear that."

She nodded and gripped her coffee mug. The warmth filled her with an odd comfort. "But, before he died, he got in with the wrong crowd. He and three of his friends started a business together. They were flipping houses. They got investors to help front money and promised huge returns. Instead of paying the investors back, they cooked the books and took the profit for themselves."

"Wow."

She nodded. "Anthony and I had separated. He'd started letting the money get to him. Plus, he got mixed up in drugs and drinking. I kicked him out, and he was happy to go. But I found some of his company's books hidden in the false bottom of his desk drawer. I took one look at the numbers there and realized that something illegal was going on."

"What happened?"

"I confronted Anthony about it. He panicked, begged me not to tell anyone. He said he would make things right. Luckily, I caught him when he was sober. It was the first time I'd seen any sincere emotion from him in months. He was scared." The night flashed vividly in her mind. "He asked me for the books. I told him no. He made me promise not to do anything. He begged me to give him a few days."

"And did you?"

The memories came stronger now, making nausea roil in her gut. "I told him he had forty-eight hours. I let him know I didn't want to have any part of any of it, and that I especially didn't want Connor to be in danger because of Anthony's actions."

"Then what happened?" John's voice was soft, inquisitive.

Her throat ached at the memories. How much should she share? Not all of it. He couldn't handle all of it. Most people couldn't, even though she'd never tried anyone before. "Then I got a call from my husband's best friend. Anthony was in a car accident and died."

John said nothing, just waited for her to continue.

"At first they thought it was truly an accident. Then investigators realized his brake lines had been cut." She left out the part about the police thinking she was behind the tampering.

He squinted in thought. "So, let me make sure I'm putting this together correctly. His friends cut his brake lines. Maybe he told them he was going to turn himself in?"

She nodded. "That's my theory, as well. When his friends realized they were in jeopardy—and their money was in jeopardy—they took things into their own hands. They couldn't let Anthony go forward with the information."

"What happened next?"

She rubbed her hands against her jeans, trying to push back the memories. They came anyway, stronger and stronger. She licked her lips, trying to find the words. "One of his friends—one of his business partners—was a police officer named Billy Walsh. He told me that if I didn't turn over the books, Connor and I would suffer the same fate as Anthony."

"Wow."

"Wow is right. I told him I'd never give him those books, that I was going to his superior and telling him everything I knew. There was another officer at my house at the time. He didn't hear our conversation, but I wasn't alone with Billy at the time. If I had been, he would have probably killed me then and there."

John was silent, so she continued. She left out the part about Billy setting it up so it looked as though she'd cut the brake lines. Billy had worked cyber crimes before being promoted to detective of major crimes. That's how he knew how to set up internet searches on her computer. He'd even paid Samantha's mechanic to say that she'd been asking what kind of tool she would need to use to remove the brake lines the last time she'd taken her car in for a tune up. Billy had told the detective on the case that Anthony was trying to get full custody of Connor. That was Samantha's motive, he'd said.

All the evidence was stacked against her.

"A couple of things happened," she continued, skirting around all of those details. "And I knew he was telling the truth about his threat toward me. That's when I ran. I knew I had to if I wanted to keep Connor safe."

"How long ago was that?"

"A year."

"How many places?"

"This is my third."

His jaw hardened. "Did you ever think about reporting all of this to the authorities?"

"Of course I did. But I can't. Billy is a police officer."

"The FBI then?"

She rubbed her hands—now sweaty—on her jeans. "He set me up to take the fall, John. If I go to the police, the first thing they're going to do is lock me up. Then I might lose Connor. I can't risk that."

"So you're going to live in fear instead?"

"What other choice do I have?" Nausea roiled in her stomach at the thought of continually living with paranoia.

"Stay here, Samantha. I can help." His eyes looked sincere, compassionate and loyal. But every man she'd ever trusted had let her down.

She locked gazes with him, desperate to see the truth in his eyes. "Why would you do that? You hardly know me."

"My gut says I can trust you, that you're telling the truth."

Her heart softened, but only for a moment.

Then John continued. "I've learned that you never win a war by running from the enemy. You win by standing your ground and fighting for what's right."

His words made sense. Unfortunately. Still, doubt lingered in her mind.

"I also have to say that I believe in the justice system. I think you should let the police in on this."

She stood, fire rushing through her blood. "Well, I don't." At one time, she had. Then she'd met Billy. She'd learned just how quickly justice could become perverted.

John reached for her arm and pulled her back. "Where are you going to go? How are you going to support yourself?"

She sat back down but refused to put her hands over her face, like she wanted to. Instead, she kept her head raised. If she just dug a little deeper, she could find the strength to do this. "I'll figure out something. I always do."

"This is no way to live, Samantha."

He couldn't possibly understand. He just couldn't. "So instead I should get you killed? I should get myself killed? I'm no good to Connor if I'm dead. You saw how this guy operates. He sneaks in. Only that wasn't Billy. He sends men to do his dirty work. He's still living off the money he swindled from those men. He can pay people so he's never caught."

"Why didn't those men who were swindled ever come forward?"

"Because my husband and his friends were smart. They only accepted money from people they knew had something to hide. They threatened if these men reported them, they'd announce their indiscretions. So the men kept quiet. I'm pretty sure some of them are probably still making payment on that blackmail."

Silence stretched. John stared into the distance. His jaw hardened and then relaxed only to harden again. "If you continue to run, this guy will continue to track you until he finds you. You might as well let him find you, and be prepared with a plan of attack when he does."

"I'm trying to picture that playing out." None of the scenarios were pretty.

"Picture this guy walking into a cabin where he thinks you're staying. Only, to his surprise, it won't be you inside. It will be me."

The thought both thrilled and horrified her. But another stark reality remained: the risks that that would involve. "I couldn't live with myself if I did that. I can't put your life on the line."

"You're not. I am."

She shook her head. "I don't think so. That's why it's best if I just go."

She stood again and took a step toward the inside of the house to get Connor. They'd wasted enough time talking about crazy plans and ideas. Now reality set in. They needed to get moving.

John grabbed her hand. "Please, don't go."

Something in his gaze made Samantha's heart squeeze. "Why are you so intent on helping me? You barely know me."

She'd asked before but his answer had never settled in her mind. She couldn't fathom a near stranger being willing to take this risk for her, not when people she'd loved dearly had been unwilling to do so.

"I know enough. I know running isn't the answer. I know what it's like to be in Connor's shoes." He shrugged, never breaking his gaze. "Isn't that enough?"

She stood there a moment, John's fingers intertwined with hers. "You really think that plan would work? That it's a good idea?"

"It's worth a shot." He looked in the distance for a minute. "If you're up for it, I have an old coast guard buddy, the one I told you offered to come here and help me out. He's as trustworthy as you can get. I've put my life in his hands more than once."

Her problem was that at one time, she'd trusted Anthony and his friends with her life, as well. And look how that'd worked out.

"Admit it. Your plan is no better than mine."

She stared at John a moment. He still held her hand as the sun started to rise and smeared hues of orange and red and yellow across the sky. John's face came into view. She soaked in his unshaven cheeks and chin, his sincere gaze and his unfaltering features. Could John be an answer to her prayers? Or was she just making a bad situation worse?

She nibbled on her bottom lip for a moment, considering the possibilities, before saying, "So many things could go wrong."

"Things could go wrong no matter how you look at it. You might as well have someone nearby to lean on."

"I'm not good at leaning on people," she finally admitted.

John stared at her, not saying a thing. He was leaving the ball in her court, so to speak. Finally, she nodded. "I can't make any promises. But I'll stay tonight. If I feel as if my son is in danger, I'm out of here, though. I'll do whatever I have to to keep him safe."

"Like any good mother would."

She let go of his hand. "Please don't make me regret this." The vulnerability in her voice startled her.

So did John. He towered over her, at least six inches above her five-foot-six-inch frame. Something about his presence took her breath away.

She hadn't had that reaction to a man since…well, since Anthony. The breathless feelings in that relationship hadn't lasted long. They'd disintegrated after the first couple of years of her marriage. When he'd started his little company and the secrets had begun to divide them. That's when he'd begun to change.

She'd tried to stick by him. Tried to be the wife she thought she should be. She'd tried not to rely on her feelings and instead honor her commitment. Samantha never thought all of that would lead her here, though. That it would lead her to the point where she was in her life now.

Something unspoken passed between her and John. He felt it, too. Samantha had seen it in his eyes.

"Samantha, I—"

The door suddenly swung open. Samantha jolted back, far away from John. She hadn't even realized that she'd leaned forward. John had obviously done the same, because he quickly straightened, at once looking rigid and uncomfortable.

They turned toward the door. Connor stood there, his eyebrows drawn together. He seemed to sense something awkward had just passed between all of them.

"Connor, are you okay, honey?" Samantha asked, grateful for the interruption. She knew she couldn't trust anyone. The fact that she was even letting John help was a huge step forward. That was as far as it should go.

Connor nodded, his eyes sagging with sleepiness. "Just tired."

"I'll go sit with you inside. Maybe you can take a little nap."

"How about if I fix some breakfast?" John offered.

"More coffee would be great."

Too bad caffeine wouldn't make this day—or this situation—any better.

As Samantha and Connor painted the cabins that morning, John kept busy by repairing the siding. While he worked, he tried to process everything Samantha had told him. It sounded as though she'd been running from a nightmare.

He really didn't know why he wanted to help her like he did. He just knew he saw the fear in her eyes and everything else didn't matter. No one should be that scared.

Now he'd proposed a plan that would sideline his work. But keeping Samantha and Connor safe was worth it. He'd learned the importance of priorities in his life and serving people trumped meeting deadlines. Human lives were more precious than making a profit. The rest would figure itself out, even if it seemed unfathomable at the moment.

Besides, his old coast guard buddy really had offered to help him, if he needed it. He thought this situation would warrant it. John was one man. He lived on an open expanse of water. He couldn't exactly camp out in Samantha's cabin with her and Connor.

That meant he needed more men, more sets of eyes around here. In order for everything to work out, he needed to have a plan. He needed that plan now.

"Connor, be careful not to get paint on the floor," Samantha said. Her voice drifted out through an open window.

Samantha's smiling face appeared out the window a moment later.

She did have paint across her cheek and in her hair. The look was more appealing than he'd like to admit. He'd already let one woman in his life down. Why had he set himself up to let down another one? Or was he searching for redemption? He didn't know.

But he knew he had to put a lid on his attraction to Samantha. He had no room in his life for romance. He didn't even deserve another chance.

As he hammered another piece of siding, his thoughts

churned. What would Samantha think if she learned the truth about Alyssa? Would she trust him then? Probably not. That's why it was better if he kept the details of his past to himself. No need to worry her any more than she already was.

"Mr. John?" Connor asked. He popped his head out of the window.

"Yes?" He paused, hammer in the air and nail clenched between his teeth.

Now that Connor had John's attention, the boy moved his work area to the wall around the window. He was a good little worker. John had to give him that.

"Why'd you buy these old shacks anyway? Why not buy something new?"

"Connor!" Samantha turned to her son, her eyes wide and horrified.

"No, it's okay." John leaned inside, the edges of his lips curling upward. "It's a good question. The cabins are a little run down, aren't they?" He glanced around the building's interior, comforting himself with the fact that a lot of progress had been made. "I guess I just realized that life was short, Connor, and that I didn't have any time to waste."

"What did you do before?" he asked with all the innocence of an eight-year-old who had no idea the skeletons his questions could uncover.

John spotted a piece of siding that looked loose and pulled out his hammer to nail it down. "I was in the coast guard."

"That sounds cool."

"It was a very cool job, but sometimes you just need a change in life." He hit the nail a little harder than he'd intended. He hoped no one noticed.

"I wish I wouldn't have as much change in my life." Even from outside, John could see the boy frown.

Samantha's gaze met John's. He saw the pain there, saw the uncertainty as she feared she wasn't doing what was best for her son. There were no clear-cut answers for her, but John did feel certain that she wanted to make the best decisions possible for her little family. He wished he knew her better; he wished he could speak more freely about her life. But they were only beginning to get to know each other. It wasn't his place; in fact, he'd already probably overstepped his boundaries. But when his gut told him to take action, he listened.

He believed Samantha. He believed the story she told him. There was nothing about what she said that would indicate she was lying. Her gaze had been steady. Her story was consistent. In fact, he felt honored that she'd even shared the details about her past. He knew she didn't talk about the specifics surrounding that part of her life.

He grabbed his toolbox and went inside. There were some baseboards he needed to replace.

Connor picked up the conversation right where he'd left off. "The coast guard sounds cool. You got to ride in boats all day, right?"

John smiled. "Yeah, something like that. Would you like to go out on my boat sometime, Connor?"

His eyes brightened. "Yeah, that sounds fun!"

"I even have a wakeboard I can pull behind the boat that you could use. That is, if it's all right with your mom."

"Can I, Mom? Can I?"

A smile feathered across Samantha's face. "As long as you wear a life jacket."

"Yes!" Connor pulled his arm back in a fist pump. "Will you still take me fishing and crabbing sometime, Mr. John?"

John's heart warmed. He'd never considered himself a kid person. But Connor was different. The boy looked at him with a touch of admiration in his eyes. He could tell the boy wanted a father figure. John's desire to fill that spot surprised him.

Too bad he'd be terrible at it.

"I'll teach you to fish," he promised. "And crab. Maybe we'll do that when Mr. Nate and Mrs. Kylie come. How's that sound?"

"Perfect!" His eyes lit up. "Later, I might play kickball with some kids I met. They came from down the beach when you went grocery shopping." He turned toward Samantha. "Is that okay, Mom?"

"As long as you stay close," Samantha said.

Connor seemed to be fitting right in here. John wanted the boy to continue to relax, to have a normal childhood. He didn't want his life to be like his own upbringing. Everything in the end had turned out okay. But there'd still been some really hard days.

Suddenly, a shadow filled the doorway. He wasn't expecting anyone here. Not yet.

John stopped his hammer mid-air and braced himself for another confrontation.

NINE

Samantha gasped as the light dwindled from the room. Someone was here. In broad daylight. Had they come back to finish what they started?

"It's Kent Adams," the man in the doorway started. He waved a hand and his gold watch glimmered in the sunlight. "The real-estate agent."

Samantha's shoulders relaxed for a moment. Just the real estate agent. A *real* estate agent.

Right?

She had no reason to suspect he was anything more. But what was he doing here…again?

Her mind had jumped to the worst-case scenarios. This was her life. One born of paranoia and fear. It was no way to live, yet she had no idea how to change it.

John's idea would be a start. But she still wasn't confident that standing her ground would work. She could just be setting a death trap for herself and for her son. In reality, her decision to stay could even be putting John in danger. She hadn't wanted to pull anyone else into the craziness called her life. But then John had somehow convinced her that all of this was a good idea.

Her mom's words again echoed in her head. *Survivor.* Maybe surviving didn't mean running. Maybe surviving meant fighting. Maybe it was time to take back control of her life.

John stood and crossed his arms. She could tell he didn't like the real-estate agent and that he didn't take kindly to another unexpected visit. His gaze seemed to absorb the man in a way that made his boundaries—and his displeasure—clear.

Samantha appreciated how John's presence could fill a room. She could only imagine him from his coast guard days, taking charge of situations with his quiet, steady confidence. Something about the picture that formed in her mind caused her heart to squeeze. Why did she feel as if she knew John much better than she actually did? It had to be the escalation of events that had increased their bond more quickly than usual.

Or was it because their connection was beyond the ordinary? She wasn't sure. It didn't matter anyway—she didn't trust her emotions and she wasn't looking for a relationship. She simply wanted to survive.

"What can I do for you?" John asked.

Kent pulled off his aviator sunglasses, looking way too Hollywood glamorous for Smuggler's Cove. "I just happened to be on the island. I wondered if you'd thought anymore about my offer?"

John shook his head. "I'm not selling. The offer is generous, but no."

Kent frowned but his expression instantly righted, his displeasure gone and his charm reappearing. "My client is willing to up his price by twenty percent."

John's arms remained crossed and his gaze steady. "Flattering, but no. Why all the interest in this land now? It was abandoned for years, but then I buy it and someone else wants it, also? I'm trying to fill in the blanks here, but I just don't understand."

"The timing is unfortunate, I agree. My client has been searching for years for the perfect piece of real estate, and he didn't find it until now." He spread his hands behind him as if to display the bay and beaches in all their glory. "You've got a marvelous view. No one can deny that."

"I'm afraid he's going to have to keep looking. Sorry." John grabbed his hammer from the floor. "In the meantime, I've got work to do."

"My client doesn't like to take no for an answer."

John paused, his gaze icy and firm. "He's going to have to."

Kent stared at him another moment before giving a curt nod. "I see. I'll let him know. You sure you won't change your mind?"

"I think I've made that clear."

"Very well, then." He gave another nod and slid his sunglasses back on. "I'll let you continue with your day. Good luck here."

Samantha's eyes met John's. When she was sure Kent was out of earshot, she said, "Pushy, isn't he?"

John scowled in the direction where the man had gone. "You can say that again."

"I'm probably overthinking it, but he almost had undertones of a threat in his voice," she whispered. "The whole 'good luck here'? It sounded ominous."

"I caught that, too."

One more thing to keep her eyes on, Samantha thought. Was this Kent Adams who he claimed to be? Why did his client so desperately want this land? It didn't make sense, and John was right to be suspicious.

But where did that leave her? Could Kent in any way be connected with the danger she'd left behind in Texas? She couldn't make the connection, nor could she be confident that his appearance was just a coincidence.

They continued to work in silence. From the way John's jaw clenched and relaxed only to clench again, he was probably thinking about Kent. Maybe he was thinking about the mess he'd voluntarily gotten himself involved with.

She could only pray that she was making wise choices. *Protect us all, Lord. Give me wisdom. Guide me when to stay and when to run. Guard my heart.*

Guard my heart? Where had that come from? No, the only thing that needed guarding was her physical self.

When they finished patching up the front room, John rocked back on his heels and wiped his forehead. "Nothing feels better than a little hard work, does it?"

Samantha smiled. "Now that you mention it, it does feel good to put in some physical labor."

She'd been on the business side of things for a long time. But before Anthony had joined ranks with his friends, the two of them had flipped houses together. Those were some of the best days of their marriage.

John glanced at his watch. "Listen, I've got to go pick up my friend from the docks. You guys want to come? We can grab a bite to eat at Erma's beforehand. She's got the best she-crab soup around. Hands down."

"She-crab soup? Do they have he-crab soup, too? It sounds like some new superhero cartoon," Connor asked. He looked amused at his own joke.

Samantha chuckled. "It's good, Connor. Rich and creamy. Maybe you should try something new."

"I'm tired of new stuff." Connor frowned. "I'm ready for things to stay the same."

Samantha could read between the lines. Connor was tired of this lifestyle of always moving, of things always changing. She was, too. Somehow, his statement seemed to confirm that John's theory was right. They should stay here. Fight instead of flight.

"They have fish and chips, too, though," John said. "What do you say? My treat. Consider it a company bonus."

Some warm, fresh food did sound good. Finally, she nodded. "I just need to clean up a little."

"Meet me at my cabin in fifteen. Sound good?"

She nodded, hating the tingling of excitement that started in her stomach.

She had no time for romance, nor did she have any desire for it. So why did her heart speed at the thought of spending time with John? It made no sense.

The only person she wanted to think about right now was her son. Anyone else was not an option.

Samantha's gaze wandered the small restaurant. It seemed as though everyone on the island had come here for lunch. Fishermen lingered at one table. Several families were there, possibly on vacation. A group of women sat in the corner, discussing books while eating sandwiches.

Erma was a plump older woman who wore an apron and beamed when people complimented her cooking. Apparently, this place had been handed down to her from her grandfather. Broad windows stretched the back wall, giving a startling view of the bay and the docks.

The restaurant itself was on the small side. The walls were a dark brown wood paneling. Pictures of local fishermen proudly displaying their award-winning catches practically wallpapered the place. The tables were outdated with glittery veneer tops that were a direct contrast to the grungy floors and battered aqua-green plastic cushions on the chairs.

"Don't let the appearance deceive you," John said as she

observed the place for the first time. "Places that look like dives usually have the best food."

Samantha ordered the soup and a side salad, while Connor got the fish and chips, and John got a seafood platter with the soup as an appetizer. Chatter sounded around her, along with the clatter of silverware. The distinct smell of the sea floated into the room, along with the aroma of fried fish and salty fries.

Several people called out hello to John. Samantha peered out the window at the bright sunshine. In the distance, down by the docks, she spotted Kent Adams talking with some fishermen.

Strange. He didn't seem like the type who'd mingle with blue-collar workers like that.

"You know any of those guys that real estate agent's talking with?" Samantha whispered.

John stared out the window a moment before shaking his head. "I can't say I do. They're not all locals. This time of the year some of the fishermen hire out-of-towners to help out. I don't know why someone like Kent Adams would be talking to them, though."

Samantha took in the dockworkers' meaty arms, thick necks, rough dispositions. One had to be strong to do that job.

Then she remembered the man with the snake tattoo who'd attacked her in the parking lot. It would be easy for him to blend in here. Had she somehow unwittingly walked into a trap? Maybe not a trap, but had she walked right into the hands of the bad guys and been unaware?

Just then she spotted the reporter milling around the docks. He stopped by Kent and they leaned toward each other, as if conspiring. Something about seeing them together caused her spine to pinch.

Just a reporter, she reminded herself. A reporter and a real estate agent.

Trusting people could be so hard, though.

A moment later, warm, creamy soup was set in front of her. She inhaled the scent of crabmeat and seafood seasoning. Her mouth began to water.

"Smells great," she muttered.

John lifted up a quick prayer and then everyone dug in. There was something that felt way too familiar and comfortable about eating here with John. She couldn't get used to this, though. She was surprised at the fact that she would *like* to get used to this.

Maybe she was longing to settle down again, just like Connor. She'd never admitted it, but perhaps all of this moving and being afraid of putting down roots again had affected her much more than she thought.

As they ate, Connor chatted on and on about fishing and learning to bodyboard and looking for sand dollars on the shore. Samantha let him talk, grateful that she didn't have to carry the conversation. For a moment, and just a moment, she blended in and felt as if she was at home.

"Samantha? Is that you?"

She swung her gaze upward at the new voice. Her eyes widened when she spotted a familiar face there. A face she hadn't seen in a very long time. "Sarah Stewart?"

If Samantha had thought a little faster, she might have denied who she was, said she was someone who had "twins" everywhere. But she hadn't. Now she was eye to eye with one of her old friends from Texas.

Anxiety curled around her lungs and squeezed all the air out.

"I hardly recognized you!" Sarah had always been outgoing and enthusiastic. She obviously hadn't changed. She spoke loudly enough that it seemed as if everyone in the restaurant turned to listen. "Your hair looks so different, but I like it lighter and longer. It's been forever!"

Samantha's throat burned, and she prayed that people would stop listening. The last thing she wanted was to bring attention to herself. "It has been."

Sarah's gaze scanned the table and stopped at her son. She gasped, no doubt for the dramatic effect. "Connor has gotten so big. Where has all the time gone? How long has it been? Four years?"

Samantha nodded. "Probably."

Sarah turned toward John. "And who is this?"

Samantha's face burned. She heard the implications in Sarah's voice. She obviously thought that she and John were together. Nothing was further from the truth. "This is my boss."

John stood and extended his hand. "I'm John."

Sarah's face lit up with pleasure. "Great to meet you, John."

"I'm restoring the old fishing cabins on the eastern side of the island," he explained.

"Oh, of course! I heard about that. It's about time someone saw those cabins for what they're worth. I wish you the best with that project." Sarah turned back to Samantha. "What brings you here, old friend? The last thing I expected was to run into someone from Texas here on Smuggler's Cove. To say we're off the beaten path is an exaggeration. There is no beaten path leading here." She laughed at her own joke.

"I just needed a change of pace," Samantha managed to get out. "I always remembered you talking about growing up here. But I didn't realize you'd moved back. I thought you were in New Jersey."

"We were, and I hated it there. It was just too fast-paced for my taste, you know? So Justin is still working up there, but I moved back to my parents' old place here just about a year ago. I missed island life. Justin comes home on weekends."

Didn't Sarah know about the pending murder charges against Samantha? If so, why wasn't she acting more suspicious? Of course, she'd left long before everything happened. Certainly she kept up with people down in Texas, though. She had to have heard that Anthony died, that Samantha had been accused of the crime.

"Hard to believe the news about Ted and Stan, huh?" Sarah leaned against the table, in no hurry to leave.

Ted and Stan were the other two men involved in the embezzling scheme.

Samantha tensed again. Had they been arrested? Had they jumped on board with Billy and claimed Samantha was guilty? Familiar apprehension threatened to take over Samantha's body, but somehow she held the emotion at bay.

She shoved her soup away, her appetite gone. "No, I haven't talked to them in forever. What's going on?"

"Ted had a heart attack and died. Three weeks later, Stan was skiing in Colorado and broke his neck. Killed instantly. Isn't that crazy? Not to mention Anthony…" She shook her head. "Truth is stranger than fiction. Isn't that the saying?"

Samantha could hardly breath. Ted and Stan were dead too? That had to mean Billy covered it up. Samantha knew the truth. Billy had killed them to keep them silent.

Maybe they'd threatened to go forward with the whole story. Maybe Billy hadn't trusted them to keep their mouths shut. She had no idea. She only knew that the fight for her life had just been stepped up another notch.

Sarah leaned closer and stared at Samantha. "You look as pale as a ghost. I'm sorry. I guess I shouldn't have brought it up. I just can't believe it. Charity told me about it. She's about the only one from down there I've kept up with."

Samantha waited to see the accusation in her eyes, but there was none. Why? Something wasn't making sense here, and Samantha couldn't pinpoint what.

Sarah finally stood and flashed one of her grins. "We need to get together sometime and catch up. Maybe I'll swing by the cabins. I'm so glad to hear that someone is fixing them up. This island is too pretty for an eyesore like that."

"I agree. It's beautiful here, just like you always said it was." Samantha forced a smile.

"I'll swing by and we can set up dinner at my place. How's that sound?"

"Sounds perfect." Samantha offered a tight nod.

"I'll see you around then!"

As soon as she walked away, Samantha exchanged a glance with John. Concern saturated his gaze. Two more people connected with the scandal were dead. Plus, there was Lisa. The body count continued to add up.

Billy didn't want anything to get in the way of his money.

Samantha had the strange urge to hash things out with John. But she couldn't talk about it now. Not with Connor here and attentive.

Her thoughts shot ahead of her plans again. She should run. What if Sarah told someone back in Texas that she was here?

It probably didn't matter. Someone seemed to already know she was.

Her hands began trembling so badly that she could hardly finish her soup. She forced a smile, desperate not to make Connor anxious, desperate to appear normal.

She glanced outside at the boats. All she wanted to do

was jump into one and sail out of this town. Even better, to sail away from her troubles.

If only it were that easy.

TEN

John finished the rest of his food and wiped his mouth with the thick paper napkin. He saw the tension across Samantha's face and wished he could do something to make her feel better. Of course, there was little he could do at the moment. He didn't know who Ted or Stan were, but he'd bet they were connected with her husband.

If that were the case, the impending storm was just getting worse and worse.

Thankfully, Rich, John's coast guard friend, would be here soon. In fact, he hoped to pick him and his friend up after Samantha and Connor finished lunch here at Erma's. They could all walk back to the cabins and he'd have extra sets of eyes on the place. It was the most he could hope for at the moment.

"Your friend seemed nice," John muttered, desperate to break the silence.

Samantha's expression looked strained. He could only imagine what was going on in her head right now. "Small world, isn't it?"

What a strange coincidence that Samantha knew someone here on Smuggler's Cove. He could see her instinct to flee kick in. He could see the panic building in her.

He didn't know Sarah. He was still a relative outsider

here. He only knew the people who he'd encountered through his work. But he knew enough to know that the stakes were just raised…again.

Just then his cell phone rang. He recognized Kylie's number. "Excuse me a moment?"

Samantha nodded.

He hit Talk just as he stepped outside and away from any listening ears. He stood where he had a good view of the docks, of anyone coming or going.

"Hey, Kylie. Thanks for giving me a ring."

"What's going on?" Kylie asked.

He moved to the side as a group of tourists flooded into the restaurant. "Listen, Nate told me that an FBI agent stopped by looking for Samantha."

"That's right," Kylie confirmed.

"Do you remember his name?"

"Not off the top of my head, but he wrote it down for me, along with a phone number. He said he was out of business cards. Let me grab the paper. It's right on my desk."

Out of business cards? Convenient.

John glanced back at Samantha, satisfied that she was still safe inside. Connor munched away on his French fries, while Samantha stared out the window.

A moment later, Kylie's voice came back over the phone line. "Found it. Let's see. His name was Special Agent Walsh."

John sucked in a breath. "Walsh, you said? Did he seem legit?"

"I didn't examine his badge or anything. I probably wouldn't even know if it was legit if I looked at it, truth be told. He came again yesterday."

More alarm raced through him. "Yesterday?"

If John's gut was right, Billy Walsh was pretending to be that FBI agent. But, if that was the case, Billy couldn't be the person who'd attacked Samantha here. The only reason Billy would have paid another visit to Kylie was if he was still looking for Samantha and trying to figure out her location.

But if it wasn't Billy or one of his hired hands who'd beat up Samantha—if they were still unsure of her location— then who was responsible?

"What's going on, John?"

"I can't tell you now, Kylie. You know I would if I could."

"I know. There's just that honorable quality you have of being trustworthy and having integrity."

How could Kylie still think that? She knew about what'd happened with Alyssa. An honorable man wouldn't have gone out of town, not when there was even a remote possibility of his spouse being tracked down by a madman.

"You're the only one who blames you," Kylie said softly, as if reading his thoughts.

He cleared his throat, not wanting to talk about this. Instead, he kept the focus on Kylie and Nate. "Look, as much as I want you and Nate to come, I'm not sure this is the best time."

"Don't be ridiculous. We want to get over there and see what you're up to."

He hesitated a moment. "I don't know how safe it is, Kylie."

Plus, he didn't want to lead these guys right to Samantha.

She paused. "Okay, now you're starting to scare me a little."

He scanned the area around him, looking for a sign of trouble. Nothing set off any internal alarms.

"I'm not trying to do that. But there are some things going on here right now." He glanced back and saw Samantha and Connor standing from the table. "Listen, I've got to go. If anything else happens, will you let me know?"

"Of course."

They hung up, and John met Samantha and Connor at the door.

"Ready to get going?" he asked. He put on his most cheerful expression.

Samantha nodded, but her gaze made it obvious that she wasn't sure about anything at the moment.

He paid, and they stepped outside. He needed a moment alone to speak with her, a moment when Connor wasn't listening.

But just then, he spotted Rich in the distance, walking beside another man and waved them over. The conversation would have to wait until later.

The men heaved their duffel bags up higher on their shoulders and started toward him. John leaned in closer to Samantha, close enough that he could smell her flowery perfume.

"Stay," he whispered.

She looked up, obviously startled, and said nothing.

"Don't run," he explained. "That's what you're thinking about, isn't it?"

She pressed her lips together for a moment. "I'm thinking about my son." She glanced over at Connor who was using the curb as a balance beam several feet away.

"These guys can help." He nodded toward his friends.

"It doesn't sound like anyone can help."

"You going to run for the rest of your life?" They'd had this conversation before, but it seemed as if it were a good time to revisit it.

"It beats dying." Her voice sounded hoarse, strained.

"They'll catch you eventually. You might as well be prepared when they come. It's time to stop living in fear."

Advice he should take himself, but he didn't have time for the introspection at the moment.

Finally, Samantha nodded and met his gaze. "I'd love to stop living in fear."

His friend reached them, then. "This is my friend, Larry," Rich started. "I hope you don't mind that he came with me. I figured you could use some more help."

John could use a hand, but having a stranger on his property wasn't ideal. Still, if he was a friend of Rich's, he was probably trustworthy.

As introductions went around, John kept one eye on everyone else in the area, making sure no one suspicious was watching from the distance.

That's when he saw that reporter. He'd stopped talking to one of the dockworkers, and continually glanced up at them. When he spotted John, he quickly looked away. What was that reporter hiding? John felt certain there was more to his story than he was letting on. He'd keep an eye on him.

For now, he had to get back to the cabins. There was a lot of work to be done.

On more than one front.

Samantha was working diligently on cleaning all the walls, trying to take her mind off everything. The deaths of Ted and Stan. Anthony's death. Anthony's betrayal. The logic of staying here instead of running.

She was getting another cabin ready to stay in tonight. The plan was for her and Connor to move to a new cabin, while one of John's friends stayed in her old one. That way, if the stranger came back again, he'd be surprised to find someone else there. Someone else who was more equipped to defend himself. In order for the plan to work, they had to work quickly to clean out another cabin and make it livable. If they took too long, their plan might become obvious to anyone who happened to wander past.

This cabin was a little shabbier, but if she aired it out, and washed all of the sheets and other linens, it could be livable.

The new windows had arrived early and were sitting outside John's cabin when they'd all gotten back. John and his coast guard buddies were putting them up in this cabin now.

Samantha was grateful to work, more than happy to have some time alone to think. She continued to scrub and paint and scrape. Connor, in the meantime, was running around outside with Rusty. Voices carried in from outside.

"Rich, go head over to Cabin 4 and start on the windows there," John said.

"You got it," Rich said.

John's friends seemed decent enough. Rich was in his mid-thirties. He had blond hair, cut close to the scalp, and a stout build. Larry was Rich's friend. The man was short and thin with dark hair that was sparse on top but thick on the sides. Rich was the talkative one, and Larry seemed more quiet and brooding.

Samantha was glad they were here. They'd help the work go by faster.

Of course, if the work went by too fast, that could mean she'd be out of a job and would be looking for a new place to call home. She'd have to cross that bridge when she reached it.

John knocked at the door before stepping inside. "It would look suspicious if all of the other cabins had new windows and your old cabin didn't. We don't want to send up any red flags."

She leaned back on her heels, taking a break from

scrubbing the walls. "Smart thinking. They teach you how to do stuff like this in the coast guard?"

He smiled down at her before fiddling with a loose light socket above the dining room table. "They taught me how to apprehend drug smugglers. Does that count?"

"Maybe." She spotted another blemish on the wall and rubbed it with her cloth. "Nothing in life could prepare me for all of this."

"All things considered, I think you're doing pretty well."

It was strange how the words made her heart do a little flip. Since this whole mess, no one had come close to complimenting her on the way she'd handled things—mostly because they didn't know anything about her past, she supposed. But whenever she thought about the situation she was in, all she felt like was a failure.

"Did I say something wrong?" John asked.

She shook her head, pausing again. "No, not at all. I was just thinking how words have such a healing power. I wake up every day feeling as if I've made a mess of things, wondering what I could have done differently, wondering why I didn't see what Anthony and his friends were up to before I did."

"Don't we all have moments in life when we think that? Of course, if we knew then what we did now, we'd change things. But hindsight can keep us humble." He pulled out a screwdriver and tightened the plate against the ceiling until the light didn't jiggle anymore.

A million questions floated through her mind about John. Why was John really here on Smuggler's Cove? Usually, she found, big life changes were set in motion by events that altered a person's outlook on the future. What was his story?

She made it a point to never ask people about their personal life. Mostly, because she didn't want people to ask about her. Not even her coworkers or those she went to church with. No, she kept to herself and figured it was better that way. The fewer people that knew her, the safer she felt.

Then she'd met John and somehow her entire story had poured out.

And, for a very brief moment, she'd wondered what it would be like to have a future with the man.

Now *that* had been a crazy thought.

Even if her life was normal—if a crazy, money hungry man wasn't desperate to kill her—she'd only known John a few days. Not nearly long enough to entertain thoughts of happily-ever-after.

"Connor seems to be adjusting well to island life." John effortlessly changed the subject as he moved on to check another ceiling light.

"He is. That's in part thanks to Rusty. He loves the dog." Rusty had been all Connor wanted to talk about lately, and that was fine with Samantha. At least he wasn't complaining about being here anymore.

"Rusty loves him, too. He's a good dog."

"Speaking of Connor, did he ask about your bruises?"

Samantha's throat ached at the thought. "He did. I tried to explain that I'd fallen. I didn't mention that I fell because I'd been pushed."

Before their conversation could go any further, an explosion sounded outside. The cabin walls shook from the force.

Samantha jumped to her feet.

All she could think about was Connor.

She rushed toward the door, but John pushed in front of her. As soon as her feet hit the porch, she saw the smoke billowing from her old cabin. Through the flames, someone staggered out of the front door and collapsed on the sand in front of the cabin.

Rich. He was alive. Thank goodness.

John ran toward him.

Samantha's gaze swerved wildly. Where was her son?

"Connor!" she shouted. Certainly he wasn't in the cabin. There was no reason he should have been. But knowing Connor...

Please, Lord, don't let him be in the cabin.

A dog barked in the distance. She turned and saw Rusty and Connor running toward her along the shoreline. She ran in their direction, meeting them in the middle, and greeted her son with a bear hug. She didn't want to let go—ever.

But she did pull back and stare into her son's wide, confused eyes. Even though he'd obviously been far away, Samantha still took Connor's face into her hands, soaking him in just to make sure he was okay.

"What happened?" he asked. He stared at the flames behind her.

"I don't know," Samantha said. "There was an explosion. Something blew up. Our...our old cabin."

She kept him in her arms and turned to look at the flames shooting from the house. Fire reached from the windows. Black smoke billowed. The intense heat devoured the wood.

The truth started to seep in. That explosion had been meant for her.

Someone had been waiting for her and John to leave. As soon as the time was right, they'd sneaked inside and set up the cabin to explode, hoping she would be inside when it happened. Lives were expendable to the person behind this act.

Now a man had almost died. Rich could have died. From the looks of it, he *should* have died.

John bent over the man now. Rich was moving. That had to be a good sign. Meanwhile, Larry had a cell phone to his ear.

As Rich sat up, John ran over and grabbed the water hose. He began dousing the flames.

With all the bases covered, Samantha pulled Connor into another hug. He remained stiff. Certainly he didn't understand the implications of the explosion. She'd tried to protect him from the dark realities. The time was coming when he'd have to know the truth—at least part of it. She dreaded that day. She wanted his childhood to be innocent and full of dreams.

"Mr. John is coming," Connor mumbled.

Samantha pulled back and turned toward her boss. His steps looked heavy across the sand, but not as heavy as his gaze. Certainly he was having second thoughts about her being here now. He had to be wishing that he hadn't talked her into staying. Anyone in his or her right mind would.

"Is Rich okay?" she rushed. She stood, but her hand still gripped Connor's shoulder.

"He's going to be fine," John started. He stopped in front of her, his hands on his hips. "Thankfully, he was at the other end of the house when the explosion happened."

Concern laced his eyes. She'd expected regret, resentment, maybe even anger toward Samantha. This whole thing felt as if it were her fault. She never should have gotten involved. She never should have looked at those books, threatened to turn Anthony and his friends in. Maybe if she hadn't done that, none of this would have happened.

Yet, there was still a part of her that knew she'd done the right thing. Anthony and his friends had cheated rich men out of their fortunes. There was something incredibly wrong about that.

She looked at the cabin, saw that the flames were calming down, and then glanced at Connor. "Why don't you go throw sticks for Rusty again, Connor? Just stay on that side of the shoreline, away from the flames, okay?"

"Sure thing." He took off, sand flying behind him, Rusty at his heels.

Samantha looked up at John, unsure where to start even. "A bomb?"

John shook his head. "Rich didn't see anything to indicate that. I'm sure the authorities will come and investigate." He squeezed her arm. His touch sent a tingle down her spine. "You okay?"

"Just shaken. That was meant for me. I'm sure of it."

"You might be right." He looked into the distance, his gaze hard and his jaw clenched.

She knew there wasn't much time to talk. People from town would be showing up soon, along with the sheriff and everyone else around. That's why she got right to the point.

"It's not safe here, John. Not just for me. For anyone." Since he wouldn't say it, she would.

His eyes met hers again, determination welling from their depths. "I'll make sure you're safe."

Samantha couldn't fathom how he intended on keeping that promise. The man's cabin had just exploded. What could he possibly do to prevent other things like this from occurring? That's why she had to remain on guard.

"Why are you so kind?"

He looked in the distance and rubbed his jaw for a moment. Finally, he looked at her again. The intensity in his eyes jolted her.

"You want to know why I joined the coast guard?"

"Sure." Her voice was soft, almost uncertain.

"I wanted to help see justice served. I wanted to help those who couldn't help themselves, whether they were a stranded boater or someone lost at sea. I've saved plenty of strangers before. I've risked my life for people I knew far less than I know you. Living to protect others is a mind-set, it's a lifestyle and something I can't easily get out of my blood."

Her throat burned again. "I see." Something about his level of selflessness warmed her.

Anthony had never been about putting others above himself. If he had been, he wouldn't have put Connor and her in the situation they were in now. No, he often chose to spend weekends with his friends unwinding. He took golf trips, weekends in Vegas, spent far too many evenings watching football.

Her marriage had been a lonely one. She'd tried to stick it out, though. She'd tried to be strong.

"Kylie and Nate trust me." John's voice broke her from her thoughts. "I hope you know that you can, too."

The thing was that she really wanted to. And she couldn't remember the last time she'd felt that way. The desire scared her more than it comforted her. Samantha tried to say something, to nod, to do something. Instead, she just stared.

Finally, John pointed behind him. "The sheriff's here. We'll talk more later."

Samantha tried to keep herself occupied while the sheriff was there by working on the other cabins. She tried to douse the memories of the explosion from her mind. But nothing would rid her of the images that flooded her thoughts every time she closed her eyes.

She glanced out the window in time to see John walking toward her while the sheriff walked away. A measure of relief filled her. She stood and stepped outside toward John, anxious to hear what he had to say.

"It appears there was a gas leak in the cabin," John started. "At least, that's how it seems, based on the sheriff's experience. He can't confirm whether the leak was accidental or if the line had been tampered with."

"Does the sheriff have any experience with this?"

"He was a detective up in…Baltimore, I think, before coming here. But he's going to have the state police check things out. They have experts who can come out and investigate these kinds of incidents."

Samantha didn't need an investigation to tell her what she already knew. Someone had found her. They would continue to try and kill her until they succeeded.

"I have to run to town and do something for a moment. Rich and Larry will be here."

"I promised Connor I'd take him into town for some ice cream."

"How about if I meet you there? Take Larry with you, though, just to be safe."

Samantha nodded. "I'm just going to finish up here first."

As the sun was beginning to set, Samantha finished scrubbing the last bit of floor space in her new cabin. John had patched up a few rough areas on the walls earlier and she was eager to get this cabin in shape. Samantha pulled all of the linens in from where they hung on the porch railing and made the beds. Finally the place seemed livable.

Despite that, she had a feeling she wouldn't be getting any sleep tonight. Not with everything that had already happened. She frowned as the explosion echoed in her mind.

Poor Rich. Thankfully, he was okay. Things could have turned out much worse. He had some cuts, but nothing had been broken. The blast had literally blown him out of the house.

Samantha cleaned up and then grabbed her purse. She found Connor outside and motioned him to come to her. He jogged across the sand to join her. Her gaze scanned the rest of the area.

She spotted John's friends sitting on the porch of Cabin 2 with cold drinks in their hands. Rich waved her way.

John had asked Samantha to let Larry escort her, but, as she glanced over at him now, she realized that Rich needed help more than she did. Certainly she and Connor could handle a walk by themselves. It wasn't even a mile.

She waved back at the two men, her mind made up, and began heading toward town.

The first part of the walk included a wooded road. The island was sparsely populated, but this side was the most spread out. After they cleared the live oak trees, they'd come to a row of houses and Samantha would be able to breathe easier.

Connor chatted on and on about Rusty, about some shells he'd found and about a little boy he'd met at the beach today.

It was good to see the incident with the explosion hadn't affected him too much. He seemed happy—something that was long overdue.

It wasn't that he'd been unhappy when they were living in Yorktown. Though they'd only been here a few days, Samantha couldn't remember Connor ever entertaining himself this easily. He'd really taken to the beach.

Somewhere in the trees, Samantha heard a crack. She glanced over her shoulder, trying not to show her fear to Connor. What had that sound been? An animal? Or worse…had someone been there?

She saw nothing, only trees and underbrush. Nothing that would set off any alarms.

But she could hardly concentrate on what Connor was saying. She listened for another telltale sign that someone might be there, might be mirroring her moves or hiding out, just waiting to strike.

No, she was just being silly.

Then she heard another branch break.

Her gaze darted around, but she saw no one.

"Mom?" Connor asked.

She gripped his arm. "Did you hear that?"

"Hear what?" His eyebrows jerked together.

She stopped, but all she heard was a bird chirping and a squirrel traipsing through the underbrush. "It was probably nothing."

They started walking again, a little faster now, when Samantha heard the sound of something rushing out from the woods.

She looked back just in time to see a man with a black mask on. He ran straight toward them.

ELEVEN

John found he had better phone reception down at the docks than he did by his cabins. For that reason, he'd slipped away after he'd showered. He needed to make a call without Samantha knowing about it.

It was a risky move. If things turned out poorly, Samantha might never forgive him. But his gut told him his decision was the right thing to do.

"Thanks for your help, Isaac," he said.

"I'll be in touch as soon as I know something," Isaac said. "I'll catch you later."

He hung up with another one of his old coast guard friends, who now worked as a sheriff down in Texas. He wanted more information on what had happened to Samantha. The more information he was armed with, the better. His friend promised to look into John's inquiries and get back with him.

John hadn't shared too many details over the phone. He'd kept things vague and said he was looking into the case for a friend who may have been ripped off. It was the truth. Samantha had been ripped off in the ultimate way. Her husband had stripped her of her pride, crushed her heart and his actions had led to her name being run through the mud.

The thing that had perplexed him was when Samantha had run into her friend at the restaurant. Her friend—Sarah, he thought her name was—hadn't seemed the least bit suspicious. Why was that?

On the other hand, Sarah had said that two other people connected with the whole crime ring had ended up dead. Something wasn't adding up in his mind. He wanted to figure out what.

With his phone call made, he started back down the street toward the ice cream parlor. The long day was getting to him, though, and he was ready to settle in for a long, good night's rest. However, given the events of the past two nights, he figured he wouldn't be getting much shut-eye tonight.

Now that Samantha's old cabin had exploded, he needed another plan. He had no doubt that the explosion was caused by mal intent. Someone had wired something or tampered with his gas line. It was the only reason he could think of that this would have happened.

He passed by the ice cream parlor and peered inside. No Samantha and Connor yet. He'd wait a couple minutes. While he did so, the local pastor came over and chatted for a few moments. John wrapped up the conversation quickly, feeling as if he needed to get back. He didn't know what was so urgent; something in his gut seemed to prod him on, though.

Just as he reached the residential road leading to the cabins, someone practically knocked him to the ground. Two someones, for that matter.

Samantha and Connor.

They were running at him, going full speed as though a bear was chasing them or something. Samantha collided with his chest, her body jerking with adrenaline.

He grasped Samantha's arms until she made eye contact. "What's going on?"

"The man." She turned behind her and pointed. Her breaths came out in deep gasps and her eyes looked wide and too alert. Then her face went slack. Her eyes frantically scrambled as she searched her surroundings.

There was no one there. Only an empty road. There were no bicycles or golf carts or people walking.

Connor squeezed against his mom, his eyes wide. "There was a man chasing us." Sweat sprinkled across the boy's forehead and his breathing seemed shallow.

They'd both obviously been frightened.

John's gaze scanned the road again. There was no sign of danger. He pivoted, ready to search for the person who'd put this fear into Samantha and Connor. "Where'd he go?"

"I don't know. He was just right there," Samantha said, her voice trembling. She put her hands on Connor's shoulders, her protectiveness toward the boy evident as always.

"Stay right here," he ordered.

He took off in a quick jog down the road. If someone had been here, they couldn't have gotten but so far. He intended on finding them and getting some answers.

The street seemed eerily quiet, though. There was no sign of movement, no hint that anyone had been chasing Samantha and Connor. Certainly both of them weren't mistaken, though. Rows of houses lined both sides of the street. Small ditches snaked through the sandy grass in front of the homes. Bicycles were parked out front, most of them complete with baskets on the fronts or backs for easy shopping trips.

But there were no figures running away. No bushes trembling under the weight of an intruder hiding anywhere. No golf carts charging into the sunset.

Then, something to the side of the road caught his eye.

He hurried toward it and squatted down. A black sweat-shirt and a black ski mask. Interesting.

Someone *had* been chasing them.

He collected the evidence. He intended on turning it over to the sheriff. Maybe there was something here that would give them a clue as to this person's identity.

He stood, keeping an eye out for anyone suspicious.

That's when he saw the reporter messing with the water hose in his front yard.

Had the man abandoned his clothes and made it to his front yard just in time to look inconspicuous? John intended on finding out.

He stormed across the street until he reached the man. Derek looked back, flinching as John approached. He held the water hose, his knuckles white with a hard grip. He took a step back and offered a smile that looked forced. "It's John, right? How's it going?"

John observed him, looking for a sign that he'd just finished running through the woods. The man wasn't breathing fast. He wasn't covered in sweat. But he did look ill-at-ease.

"Did you see anyone run past here?"

"Run past?" He scrunched his eyes together, twisting a button on the top of his water hose nozzle. "No, I just came out here to water the flowers. The sun's finally sink-ing low enough that it won't evaporate all of my water or scorch the roses. I'm renting the place for two weeks, but the owner had very specific instructions."

John stared at him another moment before nodding. "I see."

"Is everything okay?" He stepped back and began to spray some azalea bushes.

John shifted, crossing his arms. He needed to think carefully about his approach. Accusing the man of something he wasn't guilty of wouldn't get him very far in his search for answers. "Did you hear about my cabin exploding today?"

"It's the talk of the island. Thank goodness no one was hurt, right?"

"Absolutely. I thought I saw someone running from the scene."

Derek blanched, surprise washing over his features. "You mean, you think the explosion was on purpose? Here on sleepy little Smuggler's Cove? I thought crimes like that were reserved for the city. In fact, someone told me the worst someone had done here to break the law was to steal someone's fish, and then that only turned out to be an accident, a matter of someone grabbing an identical cooler."

"Recently there's been some vandalism, though it's usually safe here. But there's nowhere you can run where crime will ever totally leave you."

"Sounds ominous." Derek shifted, squinting against the sun for a moment. "Now that I'm thinking about it, maybe I could do an interview with you for my story? What do you think?"

"I thought you wanted to encourage people to come here to Smuggler's Cove, not scare them away. A story about suspected crime on the island wouldn't do anything for us during tourist season."

"But a feature story on an old Coastie who bought rundown cabins to restore? I think you'd be a great angle. Without the crime portion."

John felt his gaze darken. He knew there was something about this man he didn't trust. Now he realized what it was.

"I never told you I was in the coast guard."

Samantha saw John talking with Derek. She grabbed Connor's hand, and they cautiously approached the two.

When she was in earshot, she heard John mumble, "I never told you I was in the coast guard."

Derek blanched and his hand slackened on the water hose trigger. "No, you didn't."

"So, how did you know?" John stepped closer, bristling under the assumption that this man had looked into him.

Derek took a step back. He dropped the water hose and raised his hands in the air in innocence. "I was asking around about you. That's it. I promise." His gaze fluttered to Samantha, and sweat sprinkled across his brow.

"Why would you ask around about me?" John's voice was at a near growl. Samantha could see his muscles tensing. He almost reminded her of a tiger about to pounce.

Derek raised his hands higher in the air. "Look, I know that sounds bad. It's not what you think."

"Then you'd better start explaining because someone just sabotaged my property and nearly killed one of my workers. My sights are on you right now, and I've got the sheriff on speed dial." John pulled out his cell phone and held it up.

Derek shook his head quickly enough that it was obvious his anxiety was heightened. "It's like this. I always like to look for people to profile when I'm writing an article. I try to pick someone who will look good in the photos, who has an interesting story, who has a history with the place I'm writing about."

"And?" John pressed.

"And I was asking around town about who some good people might be. I remembered you guys." He glanced at Samantha and shrugged. "What can I say? You guys would make for some great photos. You're what cover stories are made of. You're naturally attractive and you're going after the American dream."

This man obviously had no idea who Samantha was.

No one had ever accused her of living the perfect life. Not even close. Especially not in the past year.

"Who'd you talk to?" John's voice was still hard.

"Lulu! I promise. That's it. She told me you were in the coast guard and had bought those cabins. She didn't know anything about you." He nodded toward Samantha.

"I don't want to have any part of your article," Samantha muttered. That would be her worst nightmare: a national magazine running her picture. She'd be leading the bad guys and the police right to her doorstep.

Derek may not be a killer, but in that sense he was totally capable of murder.

"I won't. I wouldn't post anything without your permission anyway." He shook his head. "Look, I'm new at this. I didn't mean to offend anyone. I'm just trying to write an article that will make my editor happy."

John's shoulders finally relaxed some and he took a step back. "Enjoy your stay on the island. And if you know what's best for you, don't ask any more questions. We're not interested. Got it?"

"Of course."

John motioned to them and Samantha and Connor followed him to the road. Samantha's heart was pounding in her chest as the confrontation replayed in her mind. Was Derek simply an innocent reporter bent on getting a killer story? Or was there something he wasn't telling them? Was there something he was hiding?

She wasn't sure. Of course, lately she hadn't been sure of anything.

As they started walking back down the road toward the ice cream parlor, Samantha glanced at the material in John's hands. "What's that?"

John held up the bundle. "I found it abandoned on the side of the road. Look familiar?"

She didn't have to see all of it to know the answer. "It's what the man chasing us was wearing."

"He apparently ditched this and then ran off. He could be anyone."

"You think the police can get any DNA off that?" she asked.

"That's what I'm hoping. Maybe you'll finally have some answers. We'll see, right?"

Her feet were nearly dragging across the dirt road. "That almost seems too easy. Nothing was ever easy with Billy. He was too clever."

"Don't lose hope."

She forced a smile. "I won't."

John had a lot to do with that. Without his encouragement and support, she'd be on the road right now, still looking over her shoulder constantly, still living in fear.

Truth be told, she was living in fear now. But John had given her hope that maybe there could be an end to her troubles. She prayed that would be true.

She had to remind herself to keep her distance from John. The future was so uncertain. She'd do whatever it took to protect her son. That meant, if she had to run again, she would. Her eyes were open and she'd take whatever action she had to.

For now, she'd prepare herself for what could be the fight of her life.

Thankfully, this time John's friends had been around to guard the cabins so there wouldn't be any unexpected explosions.

First though, she had to get her son some ice cream.

The night had passed and nothing had happened.

John had lain in bed awake for most of it, listening for

signs of danger. He hadn't heard anything except the wind blowing sheets of sand against the sides of the house.

After a lot of finagling that evening, they'd finally decided that Connor and Samantha would take John's cabin. He asked Rich to sleep in the living room and keep an eye open for any sign of trouble, and Larry to keep lookout from the cabin next door.

Meanwhile, John stayed in the cabin he was originally preparing for Samantha and Connor. He felt certain the intruder would go there first, especially if he'd been keeping an eye on things today. They'd given the most attention to that cabin; anyone could see that.

He got up from bed with a kink in his neck and a headache. He got dressed and stepped outside. Bright morning sunlight flooded his eyes and the scent of salty bay air filled his nostrils, bringing a certain measure of comfort with it.

He wanted to head over to his cabin. He needed some coffee and maybe to grab one of those cream-cheese pastries he'd picked up at the bakery in town. Just the thought of the cream-cheese filling made his mouth water.

He knew that just because someone hadn't shown up last night, didn't mean their trouble was over. Far from it, most likely. He had to wait until their next move before he could take action.

Waiting had never come easily to him, but he'd learned the importance of it in his days with the coast guard.

Samantha's sweet face flashed in his mind. Her image was appearing in his thoughts far too often. He didn't deserve another chance at love. Not when his first chance had been so badly botched.

He should have been there for Alyssa more. He should have requested a desk job or a training job. But he'd done all of that too late.

The end result was that she'd died. If he'd been there for her as she'd asked, she'd probably still be alive right now. And that realization would haunt him for the rest of his life.

As he started across the sand, he stopped in his tracks.

Their intruder hadn't been silent last night after all.

There, spray-painted across the front of his cabin, were the words "This island is in trouble."

He had to get that off before rumors began flying around Smuggler's Cove.

Because rumors would only make Samantha more prone to run.

TWELVE

Samantha stood on the beach, almost in a daze. She couldn't get the image out of her mind. The picture of the dark red words slashed across the otherwise serene white plank siding of the cabin would haunt her for a long time.

In the distance, John painted over the message. A fresh coat of paint almost entirely covered the front of the cabin. He continued to stroke the brush from side to side silently. Samantha knew she should help, but she couldn't snap out of it.

Someone had clearly wanted to send a message. And send a message they had. They knew who she was and they wanted the lies about her to be known.

If they couldn't kill her physically, there were other ways to ruin her life. They could make sure she was ostracized, shunned.

John came back over, stood beside her, and looked at his work. "Can't tell anything was ever there."

"Thank you," she croaked.

"I don't think anyone saw it," John offered.

"Someone knows, John."

He frowned. There was something he wasn't telling her. Something bad.

"Samantha, there's something I need to tell you," he started.

"Okay." She braced herself.

"Someone claiming to be an FBI agent stopped by Nate and Kylie's place a couple of days ago."

The blood drained from her face. "What?"

"He said his name was Special Agent Walsh."

Her world began spinning. Before she sank to the ground, John grabbed her arm.

"Take a deep breath."

Deep breaths would not help her right now. Billy was in the FBI now? If that was the case, she didn't stand a chance. No one would take her word over Billy's. He'd tell everyone that she'd cooked the books, that she'd changed the numbers to make it look as though someone else was guilty. The so-called proof she had would mean nothing. Panic began to set in.

"What did he say?" she rushed.

John's voice remained calm and soothing. "He just said he was looking for you."

She began to pace across the sand, her mind speeding toward the future. "He knows I'm here."

John gently grabbed her arm, pulling her to a stop. His eyes seemed to implore her. "You don't know that, Sam. Think about it for a minute. How would he have figured it out?"

She rubbed her forehead, trying not to look him in the eye. He was too even-keeled. He obviously didn't understand the gravity of the situation. He'd be panicked, too, if he knew Billy like she did. "I have no idea."

"Let's talk this out. Could he have traced your cell phone?"

She shook her head. If John's hand wasn't on her arm, she would probably run to the cabin and start packing right now. Staying here and remaining levelheaded was at odds with the urgency within her. "I threw it into a river. I did get a new one, but I've been careful about using it."

"Did you tell anyone where you were going?"

"No one." A headache that had started earlier now pounded harder.

John squeezed her arm. "It's going to be okay."

"I wish I could be so sure." And she wished he wasn't touching her. She'd come to appreciate his touch a little too much.

He extended his hand toward the path leading from the cabins into town. "Come on. Walk with me."

"Where are you going?" She glanced uncertainly ahead, not wanting to go, not wanting to stay. Only wanting the impossible—to be safe.

"To get some supplies from the docks. I'd feel better if you were with me."

"Let me just get Connor." She called her son over. "We need to go into town. Come on!"

Connor ran over, panting and sweaty and happy. He hadn't seen the message. John had already painted the first coat over it before he'd awoken. "Tanner wants to know if I can play kickball later. Can I? Can I?"

A small smile feathered across Samantha's lips. She was so glad that Connor had found a friend here. Tanner's family lived down the shoreline and the two boys had met while on the beach. "I'm sure that will be fine, especially if you stay close by. Take a walk with us now."

They walked down the road, Connor talking on and on. John gave him kickball tips. Everything sounded normal and happy, but Samantha knew all of that was a facade. Things could crumble at any minute. She wondered if the first stone was already beginning its descent.

"So, Nate and Kylie still want to come for a visit in a few days," John said during a break in the conversation.

She frowned. "Maybe they shouldn't come. Not with everything."

"I thought about that, also. They were going to stay overnight, but now they're going to only come for the day. Kylie's pretty stubborn sometimes. I couldn't talk her out of it."

Samantha prayed they'd be safe. She didn't want to ruin anyone else's life. There'd already been too many. If she'd just minded her own business…but it was too late to change the past.

They reached Main Street. People lolled outside of storefronts, shooting the breeze about the day, the new kind of fish coming into season and what the approaching nor'easter might mean for the island.

Today was Saturday so tourists had flooded the place, anxious to try the seafood here, to explore the waterways, to absorb a different—and slower—way of life.

Samantha shifted uncomfortably. Was it just her imagination or had some of the conversations stopped when she came closer? Was she simply paranoid after that message had been left for her?

People definitely seemed to be watching. It was because she was the new girl, she mentally told herself. But doubt still lingered in the back of her mind. It pulled at any chance of serenity that wanted to surface.

John's hand went to her arm. His touch zapped her out of her thoughts. "You okay?"

She forced a nod.

As they paused at the wharf, the scent of fish rose to meet them. Seagulls cried above them, searching for breadcrumbs and other food. In the distance, a kite stretched high in the sky.

Her spine stiffened as she noticed more people glancing her way. "Is it just my imagination or are people staring at me?"

He glanced around. "It could be because you're the new girl in town."

"Or rumor could have spread about the message left on the cabin." The weight on her chest pressed harder. "I have so many doubts about staying here, John. I couldn't live with myself if something happened to the people who were trying to help me. There's already been so much collateral damage, so to speak. So many innocent people who've been harmed, killed."

She thought specifically of her friend Lisa. She hadn't deserved to die. All she'd done was give Samantha a ride. Samantha would carry the burden of Lisa's death with her for a long time.

John grabbed her arm and pulled her to a stop. "Don't talk as though this is your fault, Samantha. You're just as innocent in all of this as anyone else who's become a victim."

The look in his eyes nearly took her breath away. "Why do you have so much faith in me? Most people would at least be a little skeptical."

"I trust my instincts."

She wanted to argue, to question him more, to convince him he was wrong. She didn't even know why. She only knew it felt safer when people remained at a distance... safer for her heart, at least.

She sucked in a sudden breath as a man rolling ropes at the docks in the distance caught her eye. She took a step back.

"What is it?" John asked.

She pointed across the way. "That man. He attacked me in the parking lot on the night before I came here."

John followed her gaze, his jaw hardening. "You're sure?"

She nodded as memories rushed back. "I'd remember that tattoo anywhere."

"Stay here."

John charged toward the dockworker. Samantha held her breath, wondering if her nightmare would come to an end. Or, in the least, if she might finally have some answers.

John stopped in front of the dockworker, a big burly man with meaty arms and a snake tattoo slithering up his neck. He was the kind of man John would hate to meet in a dark alley. "Excuse me. I heard you were giving my friend back there a hard time."

The man stopped rolling the rope and stared at him. "What are you talking about?" His voice was gritty and low.

"My friend said she had an unfortunate run-in with you in the parking lot of a grocery store a few days back." John refused to break eye contact. "You roughed her up."

He grunted. "Parking lot? Must not have been here on Smuggler's Cove since there are no cars. I haven't left the island in a week." He glanced back at Samantha. No sign of recognition or guilt flashed across his face. "And I've never seen that woman."

John wasn't ready to give up that easily, though. "You sure about that?"

He nodded toward the other men around him. "Ask anyone here on the docks. We've been especially busy the past couple weeks. My time sheet will show all the overtime I've gotten."

John tried to measure the man's words. From all indications he was telling the truth. But some people were so good at lying that they gave no telltale signs of their deceit. "Where'd you get that tattoo?" John pointed to the man's neck.

The man arched his shoulder back to reveal more of the intricate snake design. "A lot of us have them. We used to ride motorcycles together."

John could read between the lines well enough. But he didn't like the conclusions he was drawing. "A motorcycle gang?"

He shrugged and began to wrap rope into a tidy pile. His nostrils flared with every tug of the thick chord. "We didn't exactly call ourselves that."

"What did you call yourselves?"

"The Cobras." The man looked down, almost as if he was ashamed. When he glanced up again, his gaze dared John to challenge him.

John had been around scarier guys before. "Are there a lot of you Cobras around?"

"We're mostly out of Richmond. I got out a while back. Moved here. Started a new life. I may have this tattoo, but I'm not a Cobra anymore."

"They dangerous?"

The man hesitated, paused from winding up the rope a moment. "More than I would like. I don't know, man. I don't want to start any trouble. That kind of life just wasn't for me anymore. If your friend is mixed up with them, I'd caution her to stay away."

John stepped closer. "Just one more question then. People ever hire them to do hits?"

The man's face reddened. He glanced around, as if to make sure no one else had heard. "They didn't hire me, I can tell you that."

John glanced back at Samantha and saw her staring at them with her arms across her chest and her eyes wide. "Someone with a tattoo like yours almost killed my friend."

"I wish I could help. But if I start spilling any names, I'm dead." He swiped his finger across his throat. "My wife and kid, too. Do I make myself clear? I came here to start a new life."

John nodded. This man wouldn't be offering any more information. Part of John couldn't blame him, either. He knew how dangerous motorcycle gangs could be, especially ones like the Cobras. Though he'd feigned ignorance, John had heard of them before. They were scary, and they were trouble. No one would argue that. Somehow, one of their members had gotten tied up in the plot to take Samantha's life.

He hurried back to Samantha and filled her in. The lines at her forehead deepened. He prayed that keeping her here on the island was a good thing, the right thing. Sometimes facing your fears was the only way to have any peace in life.

He remembered learning that lesson while at the training academy for the coast guard. Some of the things the instructors put cadets through to become rescue swimmers seemed terrifying. Once they conquered them, they realized the anticipation was worse than the actual enactment.

The ferry pulled into port. A few minutes later, John had his paint, nails and caulk.

If only the cabins were his biggest concern at the moment.

The rest of the day and night passed uneventfully.

They'd worked on the cabins and gone to bed, never letting their guard down.

Sunday, Samantha and John went to church together. Then John took her and Connor out on his boat and showed them around Smuggler's Cove. He pointed out the largest house on the island—rumored to be owned by some government big shot who took his boat everywhere and never socialized otherwise. Then there was the canoe launch and the Uppards—the abandoned land mass that had once been inhabited.

Samantha soaked it all in.

She also didn't miss the way Connor looked at John with admiration and…hunger?…in his eyes. Her son wanted a male role model in his life, she realized. No, make that he *needed* a male role model. That was the one thing Samantha couldn't give him.

Monday came and went. Still, nothing happened. Samantha felt both relieved and paranoid. Why were there all of those attacks, just for the perpetrator to become silent? What sense did that make? Was everything calm because they were planning a bigger one?

She tried to relax, but couldn't.

At least they'd gotten a lot of work done on the cabins. That was good because Nate and Kylie had decided to keep their plans and visit.

Their boat had just pulled up to the pier thirty minutes before, and Samantha was busy preparing lunch for everyone.

She tried to look relaxed as she pulled out some bread and lunch meat. Not much of a lunch for a chef, but she hoped it would do. Besides, they were John's guests and she was just trying to help out.

Everyone else was on the porch, and Connor was running around with two-year-old Zander. The sounds outside were all so carefree, such a contrast to the chaos she was feeling inside.

Samantha nearly jumped out of her skin when she heard the front door open. She turned and saw Kylie there.

"Didn't mean to scare you." Her friend joined her at the kitchen counter. "What can I do to help?"

"You just sit. Get off your feet for a while." She nodded toward a chair behind her. Her pretty, petite friend had long brown hair that came halfway down her back and a smile that covered her whole face.

She thought back on how she'd first met her. Samantha had stopped by the restaurant when she'd run from Georgia after seeing a suspicious figure there and becoming frightened. There was a Room Available sign in the window. She'd inquired about it, and Kylie had offered her the apartment over the restaurant. They'd talked here and there, but never about anything too personal.

"I had a strange feeling you might have come here," Kylie said. "We made a point not to ask John."

"I heard about the FBI agent." Samantha sliced a tomato, trying to keep her voice casual.

"You don't have to tell me anything." She stood at the counter and began tearing lettuce leaves. "I have total faith in you."

Her words nearly brought tears to Samantha's eyes, but she pulled them back. "Thank you, Kylie. Really, it's just better if you don't know. For more than one reason." She nodded toward the table. "And really, you should sit."

"That's what Nate keeps saying, too. I'm really not that fragile. And, when I am, believe me, I'll let people know." She rubbed her belly and grinned. "This is a beautiful place. I thought John was crazy for doing this at first, but seeing these cabins now, all I see is potential."

"It's a great place," Samantha agreed. "I think it will be very successful."

"And look at you. You're like a regular handywoman, like one of those you'd see on TV, on one of those home improvement shows."

"You're kind. What they don't show you on TV is the sweat or how exhausted you are at the end of the day. That's actually the best part, though."

"Connor seems happy. He's running around out there, looking as if he's right at home."

Samantha smiled. "He is. He fought being here at first, but I really think he's come to love it. He's totally bonded with Rusty. He plays kickball as often as possible with some of the kids from town."

"He seems to get along pretty well with John, also. I saw him following him around out there."

Samantha's smile faded. "He thinks John can do no wrong."

Kylie's gaze softened. "I guess you don't agree?"

"In my experience, everyone lets you down."

"Don't lose your faith in people, Samantha. I know it's hard, but there are some worth trusting." Kylie finally did sit down and rub her belly again. She glanced around the room. "Anyway, how's it going here?"

Samantha forced a nod, unsure how to answer. "Okay."

"Look, you don't have to tell me anything, but if you ever need to talk, I just wanted to let you know that I'm here. I've been through some things myself, so I know what it's like to be scared and alone."

Samantha paused from slicing vegetables. Kylie's announcement surprised her. "Really?"

Kylie nodded. "Believe it or not, I had this crazy stalker after me. I was sent here to hide out while they tried to catch the guy. I jumped at everything and everybody."

Surprise washed through Samantha. "What happened?"

"They finally caught him and I put all of it behind me."

She paused and turned from the counter to face Kylie. "Did you ever just want to keep running?"

"Every day. But eventually, trouble will catch up with

you. You might as well be prepared when it does." She paused and smiled softly, compassionately. "I had a happy ending. I met Nate and life couldn't be better. The process is hard, but you just have to keep your eyes on the final outcome."

Samantha crossed her arms over her chest and stared out the window. In the distance, she could see John and her heart thumped an extra beat. "I'm afraid I'm going to get someone else killed."

"John knows what he's doing. He was one of the coast guard's best…until the fire. That's been crippling him." She frowned, then glanced around the cabin again. "But I think this place is good for him. It's going to help restore his soul."

"The fire?" Her curiosity spiked.

Kylie paused. "He didn't tell you about Alyssa?"

Samantha shook her head, knowing one of those missing puzzle pieces concerning John's life was close enough to snap in place.

Kylie nibbled on her lip for a moment. "Give him time. It's his story to share, not mine. But once you hear, you'll understand him a lot better. He pushed away from a lot of people afterward, and I think he still blames himself. No one else does, though."

Samantha stored the information away in the back of her mind. What exactly was John's story? She guessed she'd have to wait before finding out, which surprisingly disappointed her. She told herself she didn't care, but she knew she did.

Just then John, Nate, and the kids flooded inside.

A vision of a summer picnic with friends and family filled her thoughts. Warmth spread through her, but she quickly pushed the images away. For the first time in months, her heart was gravitating toward hope. She couldn't afford to get her hopes up now, though. There was still too much at stake, too much on the line.

She didn't know when one of Billy's men would strike next. She had to be careful, always watching and on guard.

She stared at the sandwiches in front of her. Even during something that should be as simple and enjoyable as a picnic, she found herself on guard.

How much longer could she live like this?

She didn't know. And that's what scared her the most.

Samantha collected leftover paper plates and shoved them into a garbage bag. They'd laid out blankets on the shore and taken their time eating, laughing, and telling stories. They'd played Frisbee, built sandcastles and chased waves.

The picnic was actually fun. Almost too fun. For a moment, and just a moment, something had felt cozy, almost like a family outing. Samantha was quick to remind herself that it wasn't.

John was her boss. Nate and Kylie were *his* friends. Samantha was merely passing through. The only person in this group that she saw as part of her future was Connor.

"Nate and I will go get the boats ready," John said.

"I'll keep cleaning up," Samantha offered.

John paused. "Thanks for everything you're doing."

The way John said the words made Samantha's heart speed for a moment. They had been low. His voice seemed too familiar, too comfortable, as though the two of them were connected.

She cleared her throat and stepped back. "It's no problem. It's the least I can do for you and your friends." She blanched at her words. She'd chosen them on purpose to remind herself of the situation. She had to keep distance here. She had to remember that she was an outsider, and that she'd always be an outsider.

Even if John's plan worked and she escaped Billy's revenge. Even if she was finally able to feel safe again…the past year seemed to have changed the way she was programmed. Sharing her life with anyone else besides Connor wasn't a risk she was willing to take.

"Samantha…" John shifted.

She grabbed a clump of her hair and pulled it away from her face where the breeze pushed it. "Yes?"

His gaze locked with hers. "I—"

Before he could finish, Nate yelled for him at the pier.

John gave a half nod and stepped back. "I've gotta run. We'll talk later?"

She shrugged noncommittally. "Sure."

They were planning on going for a boat ride. Nate, Kylie, and Zander would be in one boat. John, Samantha, and Connor in another. They would ride around for a while before Nate and his family returned to the mainland and John and his crew returned to the island.

"While you guys get the boat ready, I'm going to go put the suntan lotion on Zander," Kylie said.

"Good idea," Samantha added. "I'll follow you in a moment."

"Can I go with Kylie to the cabin, too?" Connor asked.

Samantha glanced at Kylie, who nodded, before giving him permission. "Get your sunglasses and a dry towel. I'll be right there."

She remained on the shore, picking up the various buckets and shovels that had been left there. In the distance, John and Nate worked on the boats, preparing them for the ride.

Samantha paused for a moment and scanned the shoreline. Everything had been so pleasant for the past few days. Almost too pleasant.

Was the problem hers? Was she always waiting for the other shoe to drop?

No, her experiences had simply conditioned her. She wasn't naive enough to think Billy would leave her alone. For some reason he'd just taken a short break.

Her gut clenched. She hoped it wasn't because he was planning their final shebang. All of his small ways of trying to off her hadn't worked. What would he do next?

She grabbed the beach toys and started across the beach.

That's when something hit the sand beside her feet.

She tensed. Her heart slowed, but for only a moment, before beginning to race again. Her gaze darted throughout the area.

Where had that sound come from? What was it?

That's when something else hit the sand. Instinctively, she knew what it was. A bullet.

Someone was shooting at her.

THIRTEEN

John looked up as he primed the boat and saw Samantha's face go slack. She stood frozen on the sand, her gaze fastened in the distance. Her hand clutched her chest and her entire body seemed to tense.

He straightened, his body again going on alert. Something was wrong. Seriously wrong.

A glare in the distance caught his gaze. The sun had hit someone's glasses, he realized. As his focus narrowed, he saw a man holding a gun.

He sprang into action. "Get down!"

Even as he yelled the words, he jumped out of the boat and started across the pier. His muscles strained as he tried to reach Samantha in time. She was an open target standing there on the sand.

Finally, something clicked with her. She ducked and ran for cover. Something else hit the sand, only a few feet away from her.

John reached Samantha and used his body to shield her. He pulled her across the shore, well aware that moving could help keep them alive, that it would make it harder for the gunman to get a shot.

Out here, there was nothing to hide behind. The closest

shelter would be the cabins, but that would mean running toward the shooter.

Instead, he led Samantha into the water and pushed her behind a piling of the pier.

He could feel her heaving air into her lungs as he pressed against her. Her heart beat erratically against his arm. A tremble rushed through her.

"Are you okay?" He stood ramrod straight, all instincts on alert. He braced his arms on either side of Samantha, desperate to keep her safe.

A bullet splintered the wood piling behind them, and he gulped. Whoever was behind this shooting wasn't giving up easily.

"Connor…" Samantha whispered.

"Just stay still. We're all going to be fine."

He hoped Nate was okay, as well. His friend was smart, had good instincts. No doubt he'd hunkered down. But what about Kylie and the kids? What if they wandered back outside and right into the line of fire?

Silence stretched. Minutes ticked past. John heard nothing else. Still, he didn't loosen his grip on Samantha.

Water lapped against his legs, barnacles dug into his hand, the sun beat down on his right side.

It didn't matter. All that mattered was keeping Samantha safe.

Moments strained past. Nothing. Was it safe yet? Finally, he heard footsteps against the sand. "John, it's me. Nate."

John stepped out, still on guard. "What's going on?"

His friend stood on the shoreline, hands on his hips. "He's gone. I went after him but he got away."

"Did you get a good look at him?"

He shook his head. "He was wearing camouflage. I couldn't tell anything else about him."

"Everyone's okay in the house, right?"

"Kylie's a little shaken up, but otherwise she's fine. So are the kids."

"I was the target," Samantha muttered. "Thank goodness he didn't go after anyone else."

"Let's call the sheriff. Then, if we have time, we'll do that boat ride. Maybe getting away from this island would be best for everyone."

Four hours later, as the boat puttered toward the docks, Samantha tried to relax. She couldn't. Not after everything that had happened.

The sheriff had come. He'd seemed concerned—very concerned—over all the incidents that were happening here at the cabins. He promised to turn all of his attention to figuring out who was behind all of these acts.

Meanwhile, since Nate, Kylie and Zander had to go back anyway, John, Samantha and Connor had escorted them. Was it safe to be on the water? Samantha wasn't sure. But, right now, it didn't seem to be safe. Right now, nothing did. But at least out on the water, one could see enemies approaching. That didn't help the apprehension leave her, though.

She was tired of living in fear. As a flock of birds passed overhead, a verse from Matthew slammed into her mind. *So don't be afraid; you are worth more than many sparrows*.

She knew God was watching out for her. At least in theory she knew that. Her life hadn't felt very watched over lately.

But she realized that she was still alive. She realized God had brought people to her who'd given her a hand, who'd been willing to help out. That was something to be thankful for.

Even though she didn't always see it, even though her circumstances were hard, God still loved her and wanted what was best for her. She couldn't forget that.

Samantha wasn't sure what was more unsettling: the fact that she'd been shot at or the fact that her emotions had been churning out of control ever since John had rescued her...again.

Her body hadn't had that strong of a reaction to a man since...well, maybe ever. As much as she'd loved Anthony, especially toward the beginning of their relationship, she never remembered feeling like she did at the pier.

She was aware of John's every move, his every breath, his every heart beat. She'd wanted to grab his hand, wanted to lean into him. She wanted to trust him.

She hadn't wanted to trust a man in a very, very long time.

Right now, Nate and Kylie would trailer up their boat and go back to their normal life. As John helped Nate, Kylie waddled over to Samantha.

"Be safe, okay?" Her eyes held concern.

Samantha nodded. "People keep saying that."

"You can trust John, Samantha. He's a good man. If he ever lets you past his walls, you'll be one lucky woman. I think if anyone can get through to him, you can."

Samantha glanced back at John as he and Nate talked. "I don't think he'll ever let me in. And I'm not sure I ever want to get through. I'm better off by myself."

Kylie squeezed her arm. "I've thought that before, too, Samantha. But once you find the right man, I promise you that it *is* worth it."

Samantha swallowed so hard that it hurt. "I'll have to take your word for it, then."

"I pray you'll find out for yourself." Kylie offered a soft

smile. "If you need anything—anything at all—please let me know."

"You just take care of yourself and those two guys of yours."

"Take care, Samantha. And keep your eyes open for that big nor'easter forecasters keep saying might come down this way."

As the sun set, they zoomed through the water back to their cabins.

The cabins were starting to feel like home, Samantha realized. Against all odds, her heart was starting to feel settled…and that wasn't necessarily a good thing. Not at all.

The last thing she needed was to get too comfortable. Being comfortable meant letting down her guard.

The air was warm and balmy around them, and the water was gentle. Landscape—waterscape?—like this didn't get much more beautiful.

Her mind wandered to Billy. What if he was an FBI agent now? She wouldn't stand a chance against him. No one would take her word over his.

But if he'd found her, then why had he gone back to Kylie to question her again? Was he trying to figure out if Kylie was involved?

Samantha prayed that wasn't the case.

"What are you thinking about?" John asked as he stood behind the console, steering the boat.

Samantha shrugged. "A lot of things. But one of those is that I'm very grateful for what you did today. If you hadn't been there…"

He reached across the console and squeezed her hand. "I'm glad I was there."

"I froze," she whispered.

"Most people would." He shook his head. "Whoever that man was, he's done a lot of things. Bombs, assaulting you, spray-painting threatening messages. I'm actually a little surprised he went so far as to use a gun."

"Why's that?"

He shrugged. "It's almost as though whoever is behind this wants this to seem random. Using a gun makes it obvious that the act was deliberate, with the intentions of harm."

The truth hit her and sent cold fear racing through her veins. "So the person behind this is getting desperate."

His hand went back to the throttle. "I wish that wasn't the case."

Samantha wanted to ask more questions, wanted to talk this out more. But Connor squeezed between them, and whatever had passed between them disappeared. Samantha felt a new kind of longing well in her, though. The longing for family, for community, for more.

The more she was around John, the more that desire grew—against her wishes.

And she had no idea what to do about it.

"Can I steer?" Connor asked.

"Sure thing, buddy." John gave Samantha one last glance before he began explaining to Connor what to do.

Samantha's heart squeezed. This moment was so beautiful. And sometimes, all a person had to hold on to was a moment.

She closed her eyes and tried to ingrain this memory forever.

That evening, Samantha leaned against the porch railing of her cabin and looked out over the bay. The moon reflected off the smooth water, and the night sky with its clear, sparkling stars seemed idyllic. She heard the door close behind her and John stepped out.

"Connor's asleep. Finally. It only took three games of battleship."

Samantha smiled. Connor had convinced John to play with him when they'd gotten back. Samantha had tried to curtail her son's desires to play the game, but John had insisted that he'd wanted to. In the meantime, she'd sneaked outside to try and gather her thoughts.

"I can't thank you enough, John. Connor thinks you hung the moon."

His smile slipped as he moved beside her and leaned on the porch railing, his stance mimicking hers. "Well, I have many faults."

"I can't think of one." Had she just said that? What was she thinking? Her cheeks filled with heat.

"Believe me, Samantha. If you really knew me, you'd know how imperfect I am."

"Is that because of Alyssa?" The question slipped out and she wanted to take it back. But she couldn't, despite the panic rising in her.

His eyes narrowed and he blinked a couple of times as if in shock. "You know about Alyssa?"

She shook her head. "Not really. I've only heard her name."

He turned and stared into the water, an eerie silence falling around them. She'd overstepped her bounds, she realized. "I shouldn't have brought it up. I'm sorry."

"It's okay." He remained silent, staring ahead, a new heaviness about him.

Samantha took that as her cue to leave. She'd probably already upset him enough. Which was a shame since all he'd been was kind.

"I should—" Before she could depart, he grabbed her arm and pulled her close.

"Samantha…." His eyes seemed to implore her, a mix of hope and agony mingling there.

Her breath left her lungs and she couldn't move. Her heart beat inside her chest and she was aware of every movement, every sound. Most of all, she was entirely too aware of John.

"Yes?"

"I…" He looked at her a moment.

The next instance, she was in his arms and his lips met hers. Chemistry seemed to explode between them.

Just for a blip in time, her worries disappeared and nothing else mattered.

He pulled back and rested his forehead against hers. They both seemed to be struggling to get their heartbeats under control, to gather their emotions. Samantha rested her hands on his chest, her breaths shakier than she'd like.

Then John stepped back and let out a groan. He squeezed the skin between his eyes. "I shouldn't have done that."

Her heart stopped. His exclamation seemed to trigger something in her—the remembrance that men weren't trustworthy. For a moment, she'd forgotten. "You're right. That was a bad idea."

He looked up, his gaze tortured. "Samantha, let me explain—"

Before he could say anything else, she took a step away. "No explanations. We both know that a relationship between us would never work. There's nothing to talk about."

His gaze softened. "Is that how you feel?"

"John, every man I've ever trusted has let me down. I have no hope of that ever changing."

He started to talk, but stopped himself. He probably figured there was no use in arguing. In all likelihood, he knew her words were true and that he couldn't live up to any unspoken promises of trust. It was better this way.

She pushed herself off the railing. "Thanks for everything. Good night."

John watched her walk into her cabin and resisted the urge to ram his fist into the wood. He'd really blown that.

He'd been on the verge of begging for her trust.

Then he'd realized that she was right, she shouldn't trust him. Alyssa had, and she'd died. He'd let her down in the ultimate way. He should have been around more. He should have done more. He should have *been* more.

No amount of mourning could change that. He deserved to be alone. That kiss had been a bad idea. It didn't matter how deeply, how quickly, he'd begun to fall for Samantha. It didn't matter that she'd stirred up emotions in him that he'd thought were dormant. None of that mattered.

The only important thing was that he couldn't give her the life she deserved. Because Alyssa had died, he didn't deserve to live. In the least, he didn't deserve to live happily.

He'd protect Samantha and Connor. He'd keep them safe. But that was all he could give. Pretending as though anything else was possible would just be setting up all of them for failure.

He stormed to his cabin, scolding himself for forgetting his boundaries.

Now his heart would pay the price.

The rest of the week passed with a surprising calmness. John never let down his guard, waiting for Billy's next move. He was sure it would come.

In the meantime, the storm out in the Atlantic had stalled. It was swirling over the ocean, gaining strength with every minute. Everyone on the island was watching closely to see what the nor'easter would do. If the storm did end up coming this way, it would be a whopper. For years, people on the island had feared a big storm eroding their shoreline and wiping out most of the town. John prayed that wouldn't be the case with this storm.

He paused from putting shingles on one of the cabins and looked out at the remaining cabins. His "investment" was getting closer and closer to a payoff. The reality of how quickly that had happened still amazed him. But between everyone's hard work, everything was really coming together. Maybe that meant he wouldn't have to dip into his pension after all.

Right now, Samantha was finishing painting the outsides of the cabins. The insides were all scrubbed clean with fresh coats of paint. They would need to finish restoring some furniture, buy some new curtains and mattresses, maybe some plates. All in all, things were really shaping up.

Of course, when the cabins were done, Samantha would have no reason to stay. She'd be off, looking for the next place to hide. Maybe John should slow down this restoration process… If only he had such luxuries that he could afford to do that.

He hammered another nail into the roof. His kiss with Samantha never strayed far from his mind. He could still feel her soft lips against his. He could still smell her flowery scented shampoo.

He wished that somehow things could be different. That his past wasn't his past. That her past wasn't her past.

But, if that were the case, they never would have met.

A squeal in the distance drew his attention. He looked across the shore and saw Connor playing with his buddy, Tanner. He smiled. It was nice to hear the sound of kids playing together. At one time in his life, he'd imagined himself with a whole houseful of munchkins. He'd pictured Christmases and birthday parties and first steps.

But he shouldn't think about what could have been. Right now, all he needed to concentrate on was keeping Samantha safe. That wouldn't atone for the mistakes of his past, but it was the right thing to do. It was what he *had* to do.

It didn't matter that she'd been distant toward him ever since their kiss. It made sense that she was putting space between them. It's what anyone in their situation would do.

And sure, he missed their chats. He missed sharing dinner together. But it was better this way. It was better that they didn't get too close.

He paused from his roof work when his cell phone rang.

He glanced at the number and his heartbeat quickened.

It was his friend from Texas.

"John? I have some news for you about that case you asked me to look into. The one involving Anthony Rogers. Do you think it might have been Anthony Simon instead? All the details fit."

He'd suspected that Samantha had changed her last name. Anyone on the run would do that. "The one who died in the car accident about a year ago?" John clarified.

"That's the one," his friend said. "Hang on to your seat. This is a doozy."

FOURTEEN

Samantha stopped midstroke as she touched up a baseboard in one of the cabins. Someone was knocking at her door.

"Samantha, it's me—John."

As soon as he said the words, she put the brush down and rushed toward the door. She imagined herself with paint streaks across her cheeks or maybe even in her hair, despite the purple bandanna that she wore.

When she saw John, she sensed he had something to share. She just wasn't sure if the news was good or bad. She didn't want to allow herself to hope for a minute that good news might come her way. Instead, she blurted, "What's wrong?"

"I have something I need to tell you," John said. "Can you come outside for a moment?"

She nodded. "Of course."

She stepped onto the porch where it was a little cooler. Samantha looked up at John, curious about the light dancing in his eyes.

This was the first time he'd gone out of his way to talk to her since they'd kissed. In fact, at times it had seemed as if he was avoiding her, and the realization had caused an ache in her heart. She hadn't understood until now how much his friendship had come to mean to her.

"Something good or bad to tell me?" she finally asked.

"Good."

"I'd love some good news." It had been months since she'd gotten any news worth rejoicing over. She leaned against the wood siding behind her and waited.

He put his hands on his hips. "I contacted one of my coast guard buddies down in Texas."

She tensed even as he said the words. Where was he going with this? She wasn't sure she wanted to know. "Okay...."

He stepped closer. "Listen, I know it was a risky move, but it paid off. It turns out you're not on any Wanted lists, Samantha."

She felt the blood drain from her face. A million thoughts rushed through her mind. Most weren't good. "What do you mean?"

"My friend checked with his sources at the police department. You were cleared about three months ago, Samantha. The police aren't after you."

She stood there, speechless, trying to form the right words. When she didn't say anything, John continued.

"The police are on to Billy. He quit from the department and went on the run. He never joined the FBI."

She shook her head, her thoughts continuing to swirl at a dizzying pace. "I don't know what to say."

"Maybe that you're relieved?"

She squeezed the skin between her eyes. "What if that hadn't been the case, John? What if I was still on the list? What then? The police would have arrested me, taken Connor away." Anger rushed through her at the thought.

"I didn't tell them I knew you." His shoulders visibly tightened. "I'm on your side, Samantha."

"The police would have put it together. They would have come here, arrested me." She started pacing as worst-case scenarios rushed through her mind.

"Samantha, you've got to give me more credit than that. I called a friend, someone I trusted. I was trying to help."

"By contacting someone who's a sworn officer of the law? Friendship usually doesn't mean that much in those cases. I know all about that." Billy's face flashed through her mind.

"Samantha, I thought you'd be happy." Exasperation washed over his features. His shoulders slumped, and his eyelids sagged.

"I'd be happier if you'd just minded your business, just like I'd asked you in the first place." She closed her mouth, regretting the words as soon as they left her lips.

His face hardened. "I was trying to help. You're not under the microscope anymore, Samantha. You can turn over the information to the police and they can hunt down Billy. You're at freedom's door."

"Maybe, but Billy doesn't have anything to lose now, either. His reputation is ruined. He's probably living off all the money he stole and waiting for the precise moment to exact his revenge on me." She shook her head, feeling a headache coming on. "I need to lie down."

"Samantha…" He extended his hand but dropped it before it reached her.

She shrugged. "I don't know what to say. I know I should probably thank you, but I just can't do that right now. All I keep thinking is that I never should have trusted you."

Frustration threatened to overtake John as Samantha's words echoed in his mind.

Women were so hard to understand. Why couldn't Samantha have faith in him? He'd made the call for her own good.

That conversation had not gone as he expected. Not at all. He thought she'd be grateful.

He hit the nail with a little too much force. The wood vibrated through the board as he patched another porch. Alyssa hadn't trusted him enough, either. Her ex had sent her another threatening letter the day before John left to go out of town. She hadn't mentioned the note, probably because she hadn't wanted John to worry. Possibly she thought she had more time.

Alyssa's ex had found her that weekend and she'd died at his hands.

But no one could force others to rely on them. Some people had insurmountable walls built up around themselves. He'd built up some walls himself.

"Everything okay?"

He looked up at Rich. His friend took a long sip of water from a reusable bottle and stared at him.

"Yeah, I'm fine." He hit another nail.

"Well, have some mercy on those nails then. What did they ever do to you?"

John ignored him and continued to hammer. "Have you been keeping an eye on that reporter guy?"

His friend nodded. "He's been doing a lot of research, asking a lot of questions. But nothing suspicious. Not that I can tell. What's with all of your interest in him, anyway?"

"I just got some bad vibes from him. Someone's been behind some vandalisms in the area lately. You can never be too careful."

"That's the truth. It's just a shame that someone seems to be targeting you."

"I appreciate all of your help here. You guys have been lifesavers."

"No problem. We'll keep our eyes on things around here and get these cabins finished up. I just hope that storm doesn't come and mess up all of our hard work."

"You and me both." The storm was supposed to be a doozy. They had to finish this work quickly, board it all up, then they would most likely need to evacuate the island.

"Maybe my help here will finally make up for that time you saved my hide at the academy." His friend took a sip from his water bottle.

John had helped him with his swim finals; if Rich hadn't passed, he wouldn't have made it into the coast guard.

Something about his friend's statement made realizations start to click in his mind. Rich had been joking about repaying John for his help and finally feeling peace.

But maybe the truth was that John was trying too hard to protect Samantha because he hadn't been able to save Alyssa. Maybe subconsciously he felt like he had to somehow atone for his failure by ensuring nothing happened to anyone else.

The realization caused his spirit to sag.

Maybe it was time to come clean with Samantha. About everything. About his failures. About his need for repentance. About his inability to make things right.

He'd overstepped his boundaries, and he had to be a big enough man to admit it.

Before he could, Samantha came running toward them, a piece of paper flapping in her hand. "Did you leave this for Connor?"

"Leave what for Connor?" What was she talking about? Her level of franticness alarmed him. He tried to prepare himself for whatever she was about to say.

She held up the paper. "A note telling him to meet you to go canoeing?"

John stood, his entire body tensing as urgency rushed through him. "Not me. We've got to go find him. Now."

"Let's split up," Samantha urged, her mind racing in a million directions at once.

Connor. Not Connor. Precious, precious, Connor.

"If we split up, we can cover more ground. We'll be more likely to find—"

John grabbed her arm. "We need to stay together."

"But—" Samantha said.

He leaned toward her, his gaze intense. "Listen, someone's after you. You don't need to go anywhere alone."

She took a step back, refusing to believe that was the truth. They just needed to move. "Let's stop talking and get going. We've got to find him, John." Her voice broke with emotion.

"Rich, Larry—head to the north side of the island on my boat." He tossed them some keys. "Just in case they took off in the water, I want you to be there. We'll go to the boat launch."

He grabbed Samantha's hand, and they began sprinting down the road. In the distance, John spotted Alvin and waved him down. "We need your golf cart. I'll pay you triple whatever you get paid normally."

Alvin raised his bushy eyebrows. "Sure thing. Where ya headed?"

"Sewell's Point," John barked.

"Let's go." Alvin nodded toward the back.

John and Samantha jumped into the back of the vehicle. John pulled out his phone and dialed the sheriff.

The golf cart was the fastest transportation on the island, yet it seemed so slow, at odds with the frantic urgency pounding inside Samantha.

Connor should have known not to go anywhere without

telling Samantha. Yet, he'd probably thought it was okay if John had asked him. He thought the man was a superhero.

Connor had trusted, and now he was in trouble. Could anything good come out of relying on other people? She'd yet to see it.

They bumped down the road. Her eyes scanned every shadow, every movement, every possibility, looking for a sign of her son. Finally, the trees cleared and the bay was right ahead.

Before the golf cart even stopped, Samantha was off. She ran toward the walkway leading across the marsh grass. John pushed ahead of her.

His strides increased when he hit the sand.

"Connor!" he shouted. He sounded worried. He really did care about Connor, didn't he?

Samantha's heart rate quickened. Had he spotted her son? As soon as the dunes cleared, she frantically looked around.

She spotted Connor and Rusty near some canoes with… Kent Adams? The real estate agent?

Was he the one behind all this?

Kent spotted them and took off in the opposite direction.

"Stay with Connor!" John yelled. "And call the sheriff!"

She didn't have to be told twice. She reached her son and pulled him into her arms.

"Connor, are you okay?"

He nodded. "Yeah, Mom. I'm fine."

"I'm so glad you're okay." She held him closer.

In the distance, she saw John running with all of his might.

Please catch Kent Adams, she prayed silently. *Please catch him.*

FIFTEEN

John's leg muscles burned. The strain didn't slow him down; in fact, the burn pushed him harder. He had to reach Kent and put an end to this madness.

Anyone who lured a child away from home had to be punished…not by John, but by the proper authorities. But John had no problem with catching the man and waiting until the sheriff arrived.

His feet dug into the sand and sweat scattered across his forehead.

He climbed a dune and pushed through marsh grass. Water covered his ankles as the mucky ground suctioned his feet.

Kent's breaths were coming deeper as he sprinted in front of him. Right now, John had the advantage. He was younger, faster and stronger.

The bay appeared and Kent ran into the water. What was the man going to do? Swim? John would have him there since he'd started his career in the coast guard as a rescue swimmer.

Suddenly, Kent tripped.

His mess up gave John just enough time to catch him.

John jerked the man to his feet and held him by his collar. "Who are you working for?"

Kent's eyes widened. "I can explain. Really. Please, don't hurt me."

"Start talking."

"I wasn't going to hurt the boy," he rushed. "You've got to believe me."

"What were you trying to do then?"

"I just wanted to see if he could convince you to sell your land." His voice cracked.

"A little boy? You wanted a little boy to convince me?" He squeezed the shirt collar tighter. "You'd better keep talking, because I'm not buying this so far."

Kent raised his hands, his voice trembling. "It's not what you think! Put me down! We'll talk."

John heard footsteps behind him. He glanced over his shoulder and saw Sheriff Davis rushing his way, gun drawn.

"I'll take it from here, John. We're going to take this man down to the station. I can promise you this—I'll get some answers for you, if it's the last thing I do."

John paced back and forth in his cabin as he waited for the sheriff to come by and give him an update.

The good news was that Connor wasn't hurt. He'd said that he'd just gotten there when they'd arrived. Still, he was shaken by all of the hoopla around the incident. The boy hadn't missed the worry in everyone's eyes.

They'd had lunch, John had played another round of battleship with the boy, and then Connor had taken a nap.

At two-thirty, the sheriff knocked on the door.

Samantha looked beside herself as she rose to her feet and stared at the door. John wished he could comfort her, that he could do something to make her feel better, but he knew there was nothing that would make this situation any less grim. She probably wouldn't even want his comfort.

They'd kissed and had both realized it was a mistake.

He'd found out information on the status of her investigation, and that had also been a mistake.

All they seemed to have now was a series of slip-ups.

"Come on in, Sheriff."

Davis nodded and stepped inside. "Sorry. It took longer than I anticipated."

"We appreciate you stopping by," Samantha said quietly.

John pointed to a chair at the dining room table. "Have a seat."

The sheriff lowered himself there. "I'll just cut to the chase, since I know that's what you want to hear anyway. First of all, Kent Adams is the man's real name. He really does work for a man who'd like to purchase your land here. In fact, he'd like to purchase most of the land on the island."

John shook his head. "Who is this man?"

"I'd never heard of him before, but his name is Tom Chambers. Apparently, he's a billionaire who made his fortune in the stock market. That name doesn't ring a bell with either of you, does it?"

Samantha and John both shook their heads.

Relief washed through John. Good, he wasn't one of the men Samantha's husband had swindled. Kent Adams appeared to be unconnected to her past.

"Since this Tom Chambers came into the money, he's tried his hand at several businesses, most of which were not successful. He opened a line of gift shops. He invested in a product that only reached a few thousand in sales. He started a restaurant. Apparently, his next idea was to buy this island and open a retreat for couples."

Samantha exchanged a look with him. Finally, Samantha spoke. "Really? He was telling the truth about buying this land?"

Sheriff Davis nodded. "That's right. He had enough money that he'd basically hired this Kent guy to be his right-hand man. Somehow, Kent was convinced that if he could talk you into selling your land, everyone else might cave."

"So, why did he ask Connor to meet him?" Samantha shook her head, looking perplexed.

The sheriff let out a long sigh. "He thought that news of a possible child abduction on the island might make people rethink living here."

John shook his head. "Let me guess—he's been the one behind these vandalisms, wasn't he? He was trying to scare people."

"You got it. He claims he never wanted anyone to get hurt. At least he got caught—and just in the knick of time, as the saying goes." The sheriff stood. "He's been taken into the custody of the state police. He won't be bothering you anymore."

"Did he own up to the shooting?" John asked.

The sheriff shook his head. "He said he doesn't own a gun. State records show he doesn't have one registered. It could have been obtained illegally."

"How about the fire in the cabin?" Samantha asked. "The home invasion and assault?"

"He didn't deny it or take responsibility. My bet is that he's behind it. He did mention some kind of message that had been spray-painted on the wall of a cabin."

Samantha nodded. At least they had some answers.

But the truth remained that, while one nightmare might be behind them, an even bigger one probably loomed on the horizon.

* * *

Samantha and John had spent the rest of the evening with Connor, running on the beach and playing board games and eating popcorn.

Now, Connor was asleep and John had just fixed some coffee. He handed her a mug before sitting beside her on the couch. The cabin, with its open windows and a soft breeze rushing through, seemed perfect and idyllic at the moment.

"Thank you for your help today," Samantha started.

"I'm glad we got there when we did."

"You've been a real life saver. I don't think I can say thank you enough."

John shifted on the couch, the truth pressing down on him. He knew he had to tell Samantha the whole story of what had happened. It would solidify, for both of them, why they could never be together. The reasons went beyond the fact that Samantha didn't feel like she could trust him. "There's something I want to tell you," he started.

She leaned back, drawing her legs underneath her, and giving him her full attention. "Okay."

He shifted, hating how uncomfortable he felt, and the fact that he was going to rehash the worst moments of his life. He was scared of what Samantha might think of him when he was done. "At the coast guard base where I worked, we had this wall of fame. It's these life jackets that we wore when we rescued people from sea. There's a mark on the jackets for each life saved."

"How many marks did you have?" Samantha asked. Her fingers hugged the mug of coffee.

"Fifty-six."

Her eyebrows shot upward in admiration. "Impressive," Samantha muttered.

He shrugged. "Maybe." He didn't mention that he'd

taken top honors, saved more lives than anyone else there. It didn't matter.

The only reason he'd decided to tell Samantha these things was so that she'd realize he didn't deserve anyone's love. He'd blown it in that area. Big-time. He'd been fooling himself to think that he and Samantha could ever work together.

Not that she'd given any indication that she wanted things to work between them. In fact, she didn't seem to want a relationship, either. Yet he knew he needed to come clean, before either of their feelings grew any deeper. He needed to make it clear—just in case her feelings ever grew—that he was unavailable. Nothing anyone could do would change that.

He turned away from her eyes, from that gaze that always managed to soften his heart. "The problem is that I couldn't save the one person who meant the most to me."

"Alyssa," Samantha whispered.

He nodded. He was so accustomed to resisting the memories that it felt strange to conjure them now. He closed his eyes and let himself go back in time. "We met at Nate's restaurant, actually. She was staying in the same apartment you'd rented and had started working as a waitress there. She waited on me one night, and that was it. I finally understood what the term 'love at first sight' meant. It was as though I couldn't stop myself from loving her. It happened fast. We were engaged three months after we met that night."

"Sounds as though you were smitten." Samantha smiled, a touch of sadness in her gaze.

"Yeah, I'd definitely say that. A whirlwind relationship. That's what people called it. We were married a month later."

"That is fast."

"When you know it's the right one, you just know. Isn't that what they say? I definitely believe it. Anyway, we got married and everything was going along great. It was the happiest time of my life." It really had been. He'd looked forward to coming home to a warm smile every day. Alyssa had brought so much joy to his life.

He hung his head for a moment, the crushing disappointment he felt in himself pressing on him. "There's something you might not know about Nate and Kylie. They really feel the need to help women who might be in danger. Kylie has been there before."

Samantha nodded. "Kylie told me a little about her experiences."

John paused, the words stuck in his throat. "Alyssa was one of those women."

Samantha glanced down at her hands. "Even though I didn't say a word about my past to them, I guess they sensed that I was one, too."

He didn't say anything, only rubbed his chin. "Alyssa had been in a relationship with a man who'd become abusive. She'd tried to break things off, but he kept talking her into coming back to him. The talk quickly turned into threats. She was scared for her life. That's why she fled all the way across the country."

"What happened?" Samantha stopped drinking her coffee and waited for him to continue.

"We'd been married for about six months. She hadn't heard from her ex for almost a year at that point. She'd tried to keep tabs on what he was doing by checking out his social network profiles—she used a different name, of course, so he couldn't track her. It appeared that he was dating someone new and had moved on. We really thought it was smooth sailing ahead." Hindsight truly was twenty-twenty. If only he'd known then what he knew now.

Anger began coursing through him as he remembered the events after that.

"I had to go out of town for my job. I was doing some training down in North Carolina. It was just for a few days, but I couldn't wait to get back home. I was driving up the highway when I saw smoke in the distance. I had no idea it was coming from my home."

Samantha's eyes widened. "That's horrible."

He nodded. "Her ex had found her. He shot her, set the house on fire and then shot himself."

"Oh, John. I'm so sorry," she whispered.

He dragged his gaze to meet hers. "So now you understand why I can never be in another relationship. I let the one person I cared about the most down."

"It wasn't your fault."

He shook his head. "I should have been around."

"You couldn't possibly always be around each other."

"I let her down. I told her I'd protect her, give her a new start, a safe life. What was even worse? The coroner said she was two months pregnant. Kylie told me later that Alyssa had planned this big date night when I returned where she would announce the news."

Samantha squeezed his knee compassionately. "I can't even imagine."

"I wasn't going to tell you. But I thought you should know, especially with everything we've been through together."

"Now you're afraid of being in a relationship," she whispered.

"I'm not afraid." He shook his head, trying to figure out how to help her understand.

"That's what it sounds like to me." Her voice remained soft. "I'm not judging. I know what it's like to be scared. It causes you to act in ways outside of yourself."

He didn't want her compassion. He wanted her understanding. "I couldn't handle letting someone else down, Samantha. If that's fear, then yes, I'm scared. I call it being smart."

She set her coffee on the table, giving him her full attention. "Funny how you keep telling me how I should tackle my problems head-on instead of running away from them, but that's just what you're doing."

"It's different." He shook his head.

"Why? Because the danger I'm in is physical and the danger you're in involves your heart?"

Her gaze turned intense, lit with fire and challenge. This conversation wasn't going as he'd planned. "You wouldn't understand, Samantha."

"Maybe I don't understand exactly, John, but I do understand." She jabbed a finger into her chest. "I have a little boy whom I feel as if I've let down every day. I break his heart every time I move. I break his heart whenever I talk to him about his dad. I play this game with myself where I ask myself what I could have done differently. What if I'd found those books and just ignored them? What if I hadn't confronted Anthony about them? What if I'd never run in the first place?"

A million excuses and reasons flooded his mind. He knew he couldn't voice any of them, though. If he did, he'd be speaking to himself, just as much as Samantha. He wasn't ready for that. He couldn't acknowledge that he was doing the exact same thing as he'd advised Samantha not to do.

His situation was different.

But was it?

He stood, needing some time by himself. "I don't want to talk about this anymore. I just wanted to let you know where I was coming from. I was hoping you might understand why we would never work."

Samantha jumped to her feet, as well. He expected her to argue. Instead, her voice sounded strained. Her gaze looked uncertain.

"Oh, I understand all right. The fact is that we both like each other. The other fact is that things can never work between us. You know that. I know that. If circumstances were different, maybe. But they're not, and there's nothing we can do to change it."

"You're right," John agreed. "We see eye-to-eye on that."

"At least it's all out in the open now."

He paused, hating the strain that stretched between them. "Rich's going to be on the lookout tonight."

"Good night, then." Her voice sounded somber.

He nodded. "Good night."

It was better this way. That's what he tried to tell himself, at least. But his spirit felt heavier than it had…since Alyssa was murdered.

After John left, Samantha stoically sat on the couch. She couldn't bring herself to move. Instead, her conversation with John replayed over and over again in her head.

Knowing now what she did about Alyssa and how she'd died made Samantha realize why John always seemed to be keeping a part of himself so distant. Maybe seeing Samantha had brought back too many memories of Alyssa. It made sense. Samantha and Alyssa had both lived above The Grill. They'd both been on the run. The similarities had to jar him.

Why were relationships so complicated?

Maybe she just had to find the right relationship that

was worth fighting for. Because humans, by their nature, were complicated. Emotions were rarely simple.

She remained on the couch, any hint of sleepiness gone. She listened for any sign that something was wrong outside. It was what she'd done almost every night since she'd been here on the island.

She feared Billy coming here. She feared the police storming the cabin and arresting her. Those scenarios played in her mind. She almost welcomed the thoughts. She'd rather think of them right now than John. Because when she thought of John, she began longing for forever, and forever wasn't a possibility. She hadn't even realized that she might have entertained those thoughts. She'd known the truth—that they could never be together—all along. So why did she feel so disappointed now? Why was her heart so heavy with the truth? Just because she was attracted to the man didn't mean they had a future together.

She finally stood. She checked on Connor and then began pacing the living room.

Maybe staying on this island wasn't a good thing after all. Now that she thought about it, all of this seemed like a bad, bad idea.

But what exactly was she going to do about it?

SIXTEEN

Samantha woke up the next morning to the sound of someone knocking on her door. Apparently she had drifted to sleep again. She'd had bad dreams all night—dreams about Anthony, about getting shot, about Connor disappearing.

She'd even had a dream about John. She couldn't remember the details, only that they'd been facing each other and both had been crying.

When she woke up the first time, her heart felt as though it had been broken. Her eyes even felt swollen, as if maybe she had actually been crying. Maybe she had been.

She threw on her robe and hurried toward the door. The sunlight flooding in from outside assured her that it was daylight now, and that whoever was knocking on the door was probably safe.

"It's me. John."

With that final assurance, she opened the door.

Her heart sped when she spotted her handsome boss standing there. Rusty sat beside him. "What's going on?" She pulled her robe tighter.

"The nor'easter has changed directions. We've got to batten down the hatches, so to speak, and get back to the mainland," John said.

Samantha looked beyond John at the ominous skies in the distance. A sharp wind raked through the area, sending a smattering of sand with it.

"What can I do?" She pulled her hair away from her face, but the wind kept pushing it back.

"Help me nail some boards over the windows. If Connor wouldn't mind picking up anything stray from outside— chairs, boogie boards, sand pails, any of those things—that would be a huge help. Otherwise, they'll be blown away."

"Got it."

"Rich had to take off this morning. He had a doctor's appointment on the mainland. Said he'd been having some headaches since the explosion, so I told him he should have it checked out. Larry went with him. He said he needed to board up his house for when this storm hit. It's just the two of us today."

"Got it." She hurried back inside, woke Connor with no problems this time, and got ready. What awful timing for both Rich and Larry to be gone, but she understood their reasons.

Apparently everyone in town was scrambling. The change of course put the storm here by tonight, but they would start feeling the effects even sooner. It wasn't safe to take the small boat, so John told her people were cramming onto the ferries.

She grabbed her cell phone and scrolled through her missed calls. Only a couple of people had this number, and that was only because she'd called them. She'd missed several—make that a lot—from Hank, her old boss. He'd also left some voice mails. One had come as recently as this morning.

She hesitated before pushing Play. Her throat burned as she put the phone to her ear. Her boss's voice came on the line. "Look, Samantha. I don't know what's going on or why you aren't answering your phone. But you need to know that the police are looking for you. They think you had something to do with Lisa's death. I know you better than that. I know you couldn't ever take another life. I just wanted you to know. I hope you're safe…wherever you are."

What? She'd been implicated…again?

Panic filled her. Her lungs constricted. Her limbs trembled.

She had to get out of here. Now.

John's phone call to his friend in Texas had probably done her in. Sure, John's friend had said that Samantha had been cleared. But maybe all of that was a ruse. Maybe his friend had said that, all while getting his colleagues to come out and arrest her.

She had to leave…now.

But how would she get off this island without John? He'd want to go with her. He'd convince her that they should stay together. But that would only end with more people getting hurt. With John hurt.

At that moment, someone pounded up the steps. John.

He was probably checking to see what was taking her so long. She'd promised to help him board the windows. She stashed her suitcases out of sight before opening the door.

Just seeing John standing there made her heart do a flip. She wished things had turned out differently between them. She wished life hadn't happened to them before they met. Then maybe they would have had a chance.

But there was nothing she could do to change any of that now.

"Change of plans. I've got to head down to the docks," John said. "The sheriff just called and said someone fell into the bay. They can't find him and need my help."

She nodded. "Absolutely. Go."

His gaze tarried on her for a little longer than usual. He shifted, as though there was something he wanted to say but the words wouldn't leave his lips. "I hate to leave you alone."

She waved him off. "There's too much to do here. I'll be okay."

He stared at her another moment. She could see the emotions in his eyes, how he was torn between doing right—two different rights: protecting her or helping someone else.

"Samantha—"

Something about the way he stood there indicated he wanted to say more than she could allow herself to hear. "We'll talk later," Samantha said. "There's no time right now."

He finally nodded and took off in a jog.

She leaned against the counter as he disappeared from sight. Her heart ached. Romance or not, she cared for John. The feelings had come quickly, but deeply. John Wagner was a good man. It was too bad circumstances weren't different.

But she had to think about her son. She had to do what was best for Connor and put aside her emotions for a moment. Nothing was more important than that boy.

She scrambled to her room, knowing she had a small window of opportunity to make this plan work. She grabbed the suitcase.

She wasn't confident that this was the smartest decision she could make, but it was the only one that made sense at the moment. Running was the only thing she'd known to do since this whole ordeal had begun.

She grabbed the spare set of keys to John's boat. She'd watched him operate it before. She could figure out how to use it now.

Despite John's warning, she knew she could make it over to the mainland well before the storm got here. Then she and Connor would disappear…again.

Stepping outside, the wind whipped around her. She shielded her eyes from the sun, which peeked through a dark patch of clouds. In the distance, she spotted Connor. After looking back once more to make sure John was gone, she called for her son. As he came running over, she started toward the pier.

"What are you doing? Why do you have your suitcase?"

"We've got to get out of here, Connor." She prayed that he wouldn't take this too hard, that he would accept her decision without much complaining and arguing. It was already hard enough.

"Why? Because of the storm?"

"Partly." She kept walking, kept urging him to follow.

Instead, he dug his heels into the sand and didn't move. "I want Mr. John to come with us."

"He can't come with us now."

"I don't want to leave without him." Connor crossed his arms.

Samantha paused and bent down until face-to-face with her son. "He'll leave in good time, Connor. He'll be okay."

"I feel better when he's around." His chin quivered.

Samantha's heart thudded against her chest with a sore achiness. "I'm sorry, Connor."

The sadness disappeared and anger replaced the emotion. "You want to leave again, don't you? This isn't just because of the storm. We're not ever coming back."

Her ache deepened. "Connor, bad people are after us," she tried to explain.

"I know." He raised his chin.

She blinked. "You do?"

"I'm not stupid, Mom." His hands went to his hips defiantly.

"Connor…" she warned.

His gaze softened slightly. "Well, I'm not. I know something's wrong. But Mr. John can help."

She wished the solution were that easy, that simple. "Mr. John can't fix this one."

"Did you ask him?"

"I don't have to ask." *Because he'd tell me to stay.* She kept that part silent.

"Mom…." His eyes pleaded with her.

Her hands went to his arms. She squeezed, praying that she could somehow get her point across. "I'm sorry, Connor. I really am. But I have to keep you safe, and sometimes that means making hard choices. This is one of them. We have to get out of here. We don't have any time to waste."

"Are we ever coming back? Will I ever see Mr. John again?"

Her heart squeezed so hard she thought it might burst. "I'm not sure."

His lips pulled downward, but finally he started walking. With each step, her anxiety grew. *Please, God, give me wisdom. Because I don't feel like I know what I'm doing.*

They hadn't reached the pier when someone called out behind her. "Samantha!"

She slowly turned there on the sand and saw Derek, the travel reporter.

What was he doing here? She wasn't sure she wanted to find out.

Samantha gripped her suitcase with one hand and Connor's shoulder with the other. She forced a smile. "Yes?"

Derek drew in ragged breaths, slightly bent over, and sweat covered his forehead. He almost appeared as if he'd run all the way here. "I'm looking for a ride off the island.

I came to ask John if he was leaving early, but then I saw you." He nodded toward the water. "It looks as though you're heading out."

"That's right." She could hardly deny it. She had her suitcases in hand and was standing at the start of the pier.

"Any chance I could catch a ride with you?" He pushed his glasses up higher.

"That's not a good idea." She shook her head firmly. She had to keep moving. The storm was coming and fast.

"Please. I've really got to get off this island. I've been looking for a boat to charter all day."

"Take the ferry when it leaves later."

He grabbed her arm when she tried to step away. "Please, I've got to go. Now."

She stared at his hand until he dropped it and took a step back.

"Don't listen to him, Samantha," a new voice said.

Samantha drew in a sharp breath and looked to the side. Her eyes widened when a familiar figure came into focus, walking down the shoreline toward her. Could this moment get any stranger? Could anything else go wrong?

"Rich. What are you doing back here? I thought you left this morning."

At least he was here. At least she wasn't alone with Derek. But the most pressing matter was getting off the island. Her time was ticking away.

"I remembered something I had to tell John." He stopped between Samantha and Derek.

"Mom, can I go get my seashells?" Connor tugged at her. "Please? I worked so hard on collecting them all. They're in the drawer in my room."

Maybe it was better if her son wasn't here when she told Derek to get lost. She nodded. "Just hurry."

He took off to the cabin, sand flying behind him as his feet hit the ground.

"Look, this is really none of your business," Derek started, turning toward Rich.

"I'm making it my business. Now get out of here." Rich nodded toward the town.

"I think I'll let the lady speak for herself."

"You're not going to have the chance to hear her thoughts on the matter." Rich pulled out a gun. In one motion, he pulled the trigger and Derek collapsed to the ground. A red stain appeared on his chest.

SEVENTEEN

Samantha gasped. She started to scream but felt faint.

Rich. Not Rich. How…?

She looked in the direction Connor had gone, thankful he wasn't here right now.

"Rich," she whispered, looking up at the man John had trusted. How could he have betrayed a friend like this? "Why?"

"A man's got to do what a man's got to do."

"Killing doesn't make you more manly."

"Look, I didn't want to be in this position, but I didn't have a lot of options. Now I'm making the best of it."

"You're John's friend." She took a step back and glanced at the cabin. No sign of Connor still. It was both a relief and alarming.

"He thinks the coast guard helped turn my life around. I'd hate for him to find out the truth. Life is like that, though." He raised the gun. "Now, get in the boat. We're going for a little ride."

No way did she want to go anywhere with him. In a split second decision, she threw the keys as hard as she could. They hit the angry waves with a plop. "Sorry, that boat's not working."

He sneered and grabbed her arm, twisting it behind her. "That's okay. I have a backup plan."

She remembered John's words to her, his advice about making choices between running or staying to fight.

She decided at the moment that she'd rather fight than go anywhere with Rich.

"I have someone who wants to talk to you," Rich said.

"He'll have to come here, then." She raised her chin and jerked her arm from his grasp.

He glared back. "Is that right? You've got more guts than I thought you did. Problem is, my friend doesn't want to come here. He wants you to go to him."

"That's not happening." She took another step away, weighing her options.

"You should make this easy. Let's do it now while your son isn't watching."

"You're just going to kill me." She looked down at Derek's body. Rich wanted to kill her. That's what would happen if she stayed or if she went.

He cocked the gun. "I suggest you move."

On impulse, she swung her arm around. The gun flew from Rich's hand and hit the sand.

Rich stood there, stunned for a moment before finally coming to his senses.

As did Samantha.

She took off in a run—away from Connor. She prayed he would stay in the cabin for longer, that something would delay him.

Before the prayer finished echoing in her mind, Rich grabbed her hair. She jerked backward and landed on her side. A wave crashed over just as she hit the sand. Her head pounded dully at the impact, and she sputtered as water filled her mouth and nose.

"That wasn't a good idea," Rich muttered.

He dragged her to her feet using a fistful of her hair. Samantha cried out in pain.

"Now, go get your boy. We've got a trip to make."

"Leave Connor out of this," she grumbled through clenched teeth. Her feet dragged on the sand. Rich's hands were still entangled in her hair, making her want to whimper with pain. She wouldn't give him that satisfaction.

"We could have but then you decided to get feisty. Now get the boy." He held up his gun. He'd obviously retrieved it before chasing her down.

The look in his eyes said he had no qualms about using his weapon on her. He could have her screaming with pain until she paid for her betrayal.

She contemplating trying to kick the gun out of his hands again, but her head was still swimming. She couldn't think straight.

She tried to pull herself together as Rich dragged her across the sand toward the cabin. She didn't want Connor to freak out. She had to stay calm.

Rich shoved her onto the porch before joining her. He thrust the gun into her back, hidden so Connor wouldn't see. "Don't make any sudden moves." His breath was hot on her ear.

She swallowed hard and stepped inside. Everything appeared just as she'd left it. The fact that the house was quiet signaled to her that something was wrong.

"Connor, can you come here a moment?" she called. She tried to sound strong, but her voice trembled, giving away her fear.

Silence answered her.

Why was her son being so quiet? Was he up to something? Was he hiding?

"What's going on?" Rich growled, shoving her farther into the space.

Samantha shook her head. "I don't know. He said he was coming back to get some seashells."

"Call him again," he ordered.

Her throat ached as she opened her mouth. "Connor, where are you?"

She stood in the living room, but still heard nothing. Something was wrong. She only prayed that her son was safe.

Rich shoved her again. "Move," he ordered.

She started back toward the bedrooms. She peered inside Connor's, but there was no one there. What in the world? Where had Connor gone?

"Where is he?" Rich demanded.

"I have no idea." Hope surged in her as fear tried to take root. She hoped he'd run to safety. She feared he might do something foolish.

God, please watch over him, she prayed silently.

Rich began dragging her toward the front door. "We'll have to leave him behind, then."

"But the storm." A million worst-case scenarios rushed through her mind, causing panic to build.

He shook his head. "I know. Poor thing. Hopefully he can hug a tree or something."

"You're cruel. Heartless." *Lord, please protect my son!*

"I'm broke and desperate. There's a difference."

"In your case, not much."

He nodded toward the distance. "Come on. Let's get going. Someone is waiting to see you, and we want to be gone before John gets back. I don't like it when John gets angry. And believe me, he's crazy about you. He's not going to be happy about this."

"I'm nothing to John."

"I think we both know that's not true." He shoved her. "Now, let's get moving."

She managed to walk outside across the sand without stumbling. She was all too aware of the gun pressed into her side.

She kept fervently praying. *Lord, protect Connor. Protect John.*

In the distance, a boat pulled up to the pier. Her heart stopped for a moment when she spotted the figure inside.

Billy.

She didn't have to get any closer to recognize him. That was definitely the man who'd ruined her life. She'd recognize him anywhere.

Rich shoved her, and she fell onto the sand. He grabbed her hair again and pulled her back to her feet. "Keep moving."

She stumbled along, her mind racing, her head throbbing. How was she going to get out of this one? At least Connor was safe…for now. But what would happen after these men were finished with her? Would they go after Connor, just as a final, ruthless act?

She had to think and fast.

Rich pushed her onto the pier and before she could second-guess herself, she turned to run.

She'd made it two steps when she felt Rich grab her ankle. She landed face-first on the pier.

The next thing she knew, Rich cracked the butt of his gun against her head. Then everything went black.

John breathed a sigh of relief when they pulled the fallen dockworker out of the water. He was okay. The man's family would have their peace of mind back.

And John could return to the cabins.

He looked up and saw Connor running toward him. Alarm raced through him. Something was wrong.

He sprinted toward the boy, meeting him halfway.

"Connor, what's going on?"

"Mr. Rich just grabbed my mom."

"Rich?"

Connor nodded. "I ran and hid in the woods. I saw Mr. Rich put her in a boat with this other man and they took off."

John squatted in front of the boy. "Good work, Connor. You did the right thing. Now, listen to me. I need you to stay with your friend Tanner, okay? I'm going to go find your mom. Can you do that for me?" John had just seen Tanner and his mom, so he knew they were still here on the island.

"Can I go with you?"

"It's not safe, Connor. I need you to stay here. Understand?"

He nodded.

"Okay, then run along to Tanner's house. Take Rusty with you. I've got to go."

John watched as the boy hurried down the road to Tanner's. Rusty followed behind. Then he burst into a run. By the time he got back to the cabins, the boat where Samantha had been stowed was long gone. Making matters worse was the fact that the skies were turning darker and darker. The waters wouldn't be safe soon, maybe even before anyone had time to reach the mainland.

Two suitcases lay abandoned at the start of the pier. It almost looked like…He shook his head. Had Samantha been planning on leaving? Was she going to take off without him?

He'd have to think about that later. He didn't have time to dwell on those realizations now. Not when Samantha's life was on the line.

Something else caught his eye. Was that…Derek?

He knelt beside the man and put his finger to his neck. There was a heartbeat there—barely.

As he raced toward his boat, John pulled out his cell phone and told the sheriff what was going on. Then he jumped into his boat and took off. If he moved fast enough, maybe he could catch up with the other boat. The waves rocked the watercraft, making him lose momentum. The turbulence was only going to get worse from here.

His mind raced as the wind whipped around him. Rich was conspiring with Billy? How could his friend have done this? He'd thought more highly of him. Could money really entice people to do anything?

Anger swelled inside him. It was his fault that Samantha was in this mess. He wasn't going to have another replay of what happened with Alyssa. He didn't deserve to love again, but maybe this was his chance to atone for the mistakes of his past.

The waves crested higher and higher, making his boat rock back and forth. It wasn't safe for anyone to be on these waters.

As if to confirm his theory, lightning cracked in the distance.

Where would they have gone? To the mainland?

Any experienced boater would know they shouldn't be out right now. But he didn't know if Billy was experienced or not. Rich should know better.

If Rich had any say in this, he would get off the water. There were several barrier islands around Smuggler's Cove. Most weren't suitable for living, but several were popular with fishermen and campers who would pull their boats up to the sandy shores for a day trip.

Knowing Rich and his training, he would have tried to encourage Billy to go to one of the islands. It was a safer shot than weathering this storm out on the open water.

Another wave climbed over the bow of the boat and more water filled the hull. This wasn't good. The storm was coming, and it was coming fast. Faster than even forecasters had predicted.

John knew he should get out of the water, but he couldn't until he knew where Samantha was. He'd be no good to her dead, though. He had to weigh his options carefully.

Another bolt of lightning cracked the sky, followed by a long, low rumble of thunder. Forecasters said this storm was going to be one of the worst the area had ever seen. Strong winds, torrential downpours, deadly lightning.

As soon as the thought entered his mind, he felt the first drop of rain. Then he felt another and another. Then the entire sky seemed to open and sheets of rain began pouring down.

Water sloshed at his feet. Before long, water would fill the entire hull and he would sink.

Unless he got off this water, this bay would be his grave.

Hoping his guess was right, he navigated the boat toward the three main barrier islands between Smuggler's Cove and the mainland. Rich had to have taken Samantha to one of them.

He veered his boat toward them, praying that he'd get there in time.

When Samantha regained consciousness, she was lying in a puddle of water. Rain splattered against her skin and her head throbbed.

Everything flashed back to her. Derek being shot. Rich showing up with a gun. Billy waiting for her on the boat.

That's right. Rich had knocked her out.

She pulled an eye open.

A boat. She was on a boat.

Because of the driving rain, they obviously hadn't noticed her stirring. She needed to use that to her advantage. She pretended as though she was still knocked out. Over the spatter of the rain and the hum of the motor, she could make out a few words of the conversation in the distance.

"You really think she has the information?" Rich asked, the wind whipping around him.

"You know she does. She's going to turn it over to authorities." Billy held on to his hat as nature fought against him.

"If she's going to turn it over, why hasn't she done it yet?"

"She's been scared. But one day that fear will subside. In the meantime, she needs to pay. I've lost everything because of her," Billy shouted over the storm.

Anger surged through her. None of this was her fault. Billy was the one who'd perpetrated the plan to scam people out of their money. She'd simply found him out.

She was tired of living in fear. This was going to end today, one way or another. She would fight with everything within her to stay alive.

"We've got to get off the bay. The storm came fast," Rich shouted.

"We need to get to the mainland."

"We'll die before we do that." Rich shook his head. "You should have come earlier."

"You're the one who wanted to wait until John wandered away to help that man," Billy muttered. He was still the same arrogant and saccharinely charming man. "Brilliant on your part. You knew if someone was lost in the water that John would want to help."

More rain hit Samantha's face. It continued to fill the bottom of the boat. Soon, it would reach her mouth. The choppy, ravaging waters made her stomach feel queasy, seasick almost.

"Why don't we just throw her body in the water and be done with it?"

"That wouldn't be any fun. I need to know where the information is first." Billy grabbed the side of the boat as an especially strong wave jostled the watercraft.

Samantha slammed into the side of the boat. She fought to remain motionless, to not give any sign that she was lucid. A moment later, the two men began their shouted conversation again.

"Whatever. I'm just hired help."

Billy leveled his gaze with Rich. "You've become more than that. You've become an accomplice, whether you like it or not. You're in this. If I go down, you go down."

"Right now, we're all going to go down if we don't get off this water."

The boat rocked back and forth violently. More water lapped onto her face and thunder rumbled loudly. The open expanse of water seemed to amplify the sound so that Samantha could feel it all the way down to her bones.

All of a sudden the boat jostled. Hard.

Samantha was flung over the side of the boat. Water surrounded her. Filled her nose, her mouth.

She burst to life. She floundered a moment, desperate to get to the surface. When she broke free, she sputtered. Tried to get the water out of her lungs. Her arms flailed as a huge wave sank her.

Someone grabbed her wrist.

She fought against him, trying to tread water, trying to keep air in her lungs.

Through the haze of the rain, Billy's face came into view. He and Rich had fallen in the water, as well.

Even now, as the waves tried to drown her, he was coming after her.

Using all the strength she had, she kicked at Billy. The

motion seemed to be enough to buy her some time. He disappeared into the deep.

She began swimming, fast and furious. She knew they'd said that land wasn't too far away. But in the water, every direction appeared to be the same. She only prayed she was headed the right way. She didn't have time to think too much, though. She had to move. It was sink or swim, and she wasn't going down that easily.

She swam until her arms ached. Finally her feet hit sand.

She blinked and wiped the water from her eyes. Those might be trees in the distance. One of the barrier islands. A lone, abandoned building stood in the center.

The Uppards, she realized.

She'd reached a sandbar. Not too much farther.

She squinted against the water, trying to spot any sign of trouble. A sign of Billy or Rich.

She saw no one.

Samantha didn't know how long that would last, though. She had to hurry.

Using the last of her energy, she swam to shore and dragged herself onto land. Rain stung her eyes and she coughed, water coming from her lungs.

The trees. She had to get to the trees.

Forecasters were calling for a rising tide. This whole island could disappear under water soon, for all she knew.

Each step felt as though she was slogging through quicksand.

She couldn't go to the house. That would be the first place they'd look.

Finally, she reached a grove of live oak trees. She sank to the ground beside one of them.

Lightning cracked in the distance.

That's when she spotted someone else coming ashore.
She braced herself.
The worst wasn't over yet. Not by a long shot.

EIGHTEEN

John saw the boat remains floating in the water.

Was that the boat where Samantha had been?

Alarm rushed through him. Was she okay?

He slowed his boat and searched the water for a sign of life. Life jackets and coolers floated all around the structure.

He didn't see any bodies, no signs of death.

But capsizing in a storm like this wouldn't leave very many survivors.

He thought of Connor. Connor couldn't lose his mom. He needed her.

If John was honest with himself, *he* needed Samantha, too. The thought of life without her caused an ache to form in his chest.

He slowly puttered the boat, fighting violent waves. If there was a chance Samantha was out here, he had to stay.

A head bobbed to the surface.

John stopped his boat beside the figure.

Rich.

Reaching into the water, John pulled his so-called friend from the waves. Just as the man sprawled at the floor of his boat, the bay growled angrily. This wasn't good. The storm was getting closer. No one would survive out on this water for much longer, especially not in a small fishing vessel like this one.

"Where's Samantha?" John grabbed Rich's shirt—drenched from the rain—and made sure the man saw the intensity in his gaze.

"I don't know." Rich coughed, water gurgling in his throat. "The boat flipped. The storm. I couldn't see anything."

"Why would you do this?"

Rich shook his head, his voice now hoarse, his skin pale. "You wouldn't understand."

"I understand hard decisions. I just thought you had more backbone than that. Did you volunteer to help me because you knew Samantha was here?" The timeline didn't add up in John's mind. What was he missing?

"No, I promise you. That wasn't the case. Billy didn't approach me until a few days ago on the docks. I told him no initially, that I couldn't do that to you. But then he offered more money, money that would go a long way."

"Sounds as if you're making one bad decision after another." He didn't have time to talk about all of this now.

More water lapped over the side of the boat. He ignored the storm a minute. He needed answers. Now.

"To the mainland."

"What was Billy planning to do with Samantha?"

"He was going to torture her until she handed over some information. You don't want to mess with this guy."

Another wave lapped over the boat and it teetered. It was just a matter of time before John's boat suffered the same fate as Billy's. He had to get to the closest island and now.

Samantha remained low as she looked for the figure in the distance. Billy. Billy was on the island.

But where had he gone?

A gust of wind had peppered her eyes with sand and in that brief moment, he'd disappeared.

The island wasn't that big and a pool of water had already gathered near her feet. Unless she reached the highest point of land, she was going to be covered in water before the end of this storm. Islands like this didn't have any caves or any other means for shelter. They were basically oversize sandbars that had survived for years.

And if the storm didn't do her in, Billy would. Her options weren't looking good.

Where had he gone? She crouched behind the tree, trying to see him in the flashes of lightning. But he'd disappeared. Somehow in those dark moments when waters had been pouring like a stream from the sky, he'd vanished.

The sounds of the storm masked any telltale signs that he was getting closer. She needed to get to higher ground yet remain low in the brush at the same time.

The wind sent a branch toppling to the ground. It narrowly missed hitting her.

Her heart beat even faster.

The magnitude of the storm took her breath away, and she knew the worst wasn't even on them yet.

She squeezed her eyes shut. *Please, Lord, protect me. Help me. Give me wisdom. Watch over Connor. Keep him safe.*

As lightning flashed again, she spotted Billy. He was limping. His forehead was bleeding. And he was coming her way. Only a few feet away for that matter.

"Samantha!" he called. "I'll find you. And I'll kill you, if it's the last thing I do!"

It was a risk. John knew that. But this island seemed the most likely one where Samantha may have washed up.

He prayed he was right. Because otherwise he'd just left the woman he loved out in the bay to die.

He *loved*.

The thought seemed so foreign, yet so familiar. He had been letting his past hold him back. He had to remedy that and tell Samantha how he felt. But first he had to find her.

And he had to figure out what to do with Rich. If he tied the man up, he'd basically be handing him a death sentence. If he didn't tie him up, he'd be handing himself a death sentence.

Instead, he knocked Rich out, dragged him onto the sand, and prayed he'd remain unconscious for long enough that John could find Samantha.

He lumbered onto the sand. The rain and sand blinded him. He shielded his eyes. The downpour had erased any footprints, any sign that someone had been here. If he was going to find Samantha, it would be more like a game of hide and seek. The only sense he could use was sight. His hearing, smell, everything else was blinded by the storm raging around him.

The water around the island was already up to the dune grass. There was usually a skirt of sand around the island. That meant the water was rising rapidly. It was only a matter of time before the whole thing was under water. He had to move quickly.

This would not be a replay of Alyssa. This wouldn't be the same story, only with a flood instead of a fire.

He pushed through the brush at the center of the island. The whole place was probably only an acre, if he had to guess. There was evidence that fishermen and partyers had been out here. There were soda cans and potato chip wrappers and old fishing line. He could barely make out anything in the storm, but every once in a while, he stumbled over something. Too bad there was nothing that would give evidence that Samantha was here.

He paused as he spotted something. Was that the purple bandana that Samantha always wore? Maybe this was the right place.

Hope surged in him, renewing his search. This place wasn't that big. He could search it quickly. He wasn't sure what he'd do once he found her. Going back out on the water wouldn't be safe. Neither would staying here. But he'd cross that bridge when he got there. Right now he just had to find her.

Lightning flashed in the sky. It illuminated a figure in the distance.

Billy.

John had done his own internet search on him. He'd seen his picture.

Right now, the man had the look of a hunter searching for prey.

John ducked behind some thick underbrush. He needed to keep his eye on the man.

Because that man was obviously trying to keep his eyes open for Samantha.

Samantha heard Billy call her again.

She didn't have to look at him to know he had a crazy look in his eyes. He'd always had a bit of a crazy look about him. She'd just never realized it until she discovered his secret. Before that, she'd just thought he'd looked passionate and curious and a bit mischievous. Once she knew the truth, everything else made sense.

Billy was a psychopath. He was the scariest kind of psychopath. He was the one who could so easily conceal the truth from others, to the point where they trusted him with their lives. That's how he became a cop.

"Where are you, Samantha? You might as well give up. Make this easier on yourself. I know you're trembling with fear right now. We can put an end to all of this right here and now. You don't have to live like this anymore. In fact, you don't have to live at all."

She pressed herself against the tree, hoping he didn't see her. One flash of lightning, one wrong move could give away her location.

"You just need to face your fate, Samantha. You've known from the start that at the end of all of this, you were going to die. Aren't you tired of being scared? It's exhausting, isn't it?"

She could hardly breathe. She could hear him getting closer and closer. It was only a matter of time before he found her. Then she'd be a goner. She had nothing to defend herself with. She had nowhere to go.

The one thing she'd done right before she'd attempted to leave was putting her cell phone into a plastic bag. She'd had the foresight to know it could very well rain on her on the trip to the mainland. She wanted to keep her phone close, just in case of an emergency.

This definitely counted.

She pulled it out from her back pocket, relief washing through her when she saw a signal. The plastic bag had worked.

"Thank You, Jesus," she whispered to heaven.

She texted both John and Nate, letting them know where she kept the safe-deposit box that held all the evidence implicating Billy. At least, at the end of this, they could hopefully catch him and put him behind bars where he belonged.

That was the only positive outcome she could see.

She hoped Connor was okay.

Maybe John would take care of him like she'd ask him

to if anything happened to her. John was so good with him. And Samantha had no one else.

Though she hadn't wanted to admit it, every time she closed her eyes she'd seen images of happily-ever-after, and each one had included John. She'd tried to deny it; she'd tried to push the images away. But they'd been there. They'd warmed her heart only to leave her reeling as she'd realized that it wasn't a possibility.

With trembling hands, she pulled her phone out again. She shouldn't do this. She knew she shouldn't. But she had to tie up loose ends, and this was the only way she knew how to do that.

She texted John, asking him to look after Connor, saying she was sorry for all the trouble she'd brought upon him. She ended with, *You really came to mean a lot to me. If circumstances had been different...both of our circumstances...* Between the storm and the isolated location, she could only pray all the messages she'd sent had gone through.

Just as she hit Send, she felt a shadow fall over her.

She looked up and Billy was standing there, a gleam in his eyes and a gun in his hands.

John spotted Billy. Saw the gun.

He shifted from his barricade.

And there.

There was Samantha.

She was alive.

Thank goodness, she was alive!

But she wouldn't be for long if he didn't do something.

Before Billy could realize what was happening, John darted from his hideout. He tackled the man until they both landed on the ground with a thud.

The gun flew from Billy's hands.

"John!" Samantha gasped.

He wrestled with Billy.

She scrambled toward the gun just as Billy sat up and threw a right hook at John. John dodged him and tackled him back down. They thrashed on the wet, sopping ground, each fighting for survival.

Samantha grabbed the gun. Her hands trembled on the weapon. In one swift move, Billy kicked the firearm from her.

It scattered into a puddle. Samantha began crawling toward it.

Billy lunged, grabbed Samantha by the wrist. "Not so fast, sweetie."

Her face twisted with pain.

John grabbed him and slammed him to the ground again.

The wind beat through the trees. The sand became an obstacle within itself as it flew through the air, stinging them with its minuscule pebbles. Limbs from the trees cracked and nosedived to the ground until the wind caught them and they became projectiles. There was nothing safe about being out here. Not Billy. Not the weather. Not Samantha—at least not where his heart was concerned.

Billy, in a burst of strength, threw John off him. In one swift move, he stretched his arm and reached for the gun, pointing it at Samantha's head.

"All of this is going to end now," he shouted over the howling winds.

John raised his hands. "Don't hurt her."

"At least one man in her life has been noble and loyal." Billy sneered.

John saw a man who had nothing to lose. The police had already found him out. He was on the run. He had no reputation to tarnish—it had already been destroyed. People with nothing to lose did foolish, reckless things.

"It's not too late to turn things around. It's never too late," John urged.

"Says the one who let his wife die at the hands of an ex-boyfriend. I'm not sure how reliable you are."

"He would never do what you and Anthony and the rest of your friends did," Samantha shouted over the wind. "He's ten times the man any of you ever were. What happened to Alyssa was the fault of a man just as deranged as you are."

"It's going to be really hard on him then when you die at the hands of someone else just as deranged. Imagine the guilt he's going to carry with him. Now and forever." Billy smiled sadistically. "Unless he dies here, too. But then again, what fun would that be? It's only fun if people have to live with the consequences of their choices."

"You're sick," Samantha muttered. Despite the fear in her voice, her eyes were narrowed and filled with disgust. John also saw the worry there. That was Samantha. Always worrying about other people and how her life would affect them. There were worse qualities she could have.

"Enough of this talk. Let's get down to business."

John saw Billy's finger flex on the trigger. That's when he dove at the man, determined to save the one other woman in his life he could see himself loving forever.

Just as his body collided with Billy's, he heard a shot ring out.

His heart sank as he feared the worst.

Samantha stared at John, her breath unable to reach her lungs. What had just happened?

Billy crumpled in front of John, red staining his shirt.

Somehow, he'd ended up shooting himself, Samantha realized.

He stared into space for a moment, then his body went still.

He was dead.

In one swift move, Samantha darted across the soggy landscape and fell into John's arms.

"I'm so glad you're okay," John whispered, his breath coming in rugged gasps.

"Connor?"

"He's fine."

"Thank goodness. You shouldn't have come. How'd you know?"

"Connor saw what happened and got me."

"I'm sorry, John. Fear makes a person react in ways they wouldn't ordinarily react. I was going to run—"

"It's okay. We're together now. That's all that matters."

She pulled some more rain-slathered hair away from her eyes. The wind strengthened, sending a tree toppling close by.

"Though we're not out of the woods, yet," John muttered. "We can't risk getting back in the boat. Our chances are better here."

"Our chances aren't good period, are they?"

He said nothing. "We're going to get through this. The coast guard will send someone out, once the storm weakens some. It's too dangerous right now."

"John, look." She pointed in the distance. The water around the island had risen more. Soon, the whole island would be a part of the bay. A storm had formed it, and a storm would probably destroy it.

He grabbed her hand. "Come on. We've got to find higher ground. Then we'll hunker down. This storm is only going to get worse."

"Connor?" she asked.

"Tanner's family is watching him and Rusty. They'll be fine."

At least Connor was in a better position than she and John. He'd be safe from the storm at Tanner's. Still, the comfort of the thought didn't begin to compare to the agony she felt when thinking about never seeing him again.

They sloshed through the landscape. At one time, it probably would have seemed rugged and untouched. Now it seemed like a grave. A watery grave.

They found a patch of land that wasn't covered in water, and crouched beside a tree there. "Stay here for a minute," John told her.

"Where are you going?" She clutched his arm.

"I've got to get Rich."

"But—"

He leaned toward her, locking his gaze with hers. "I'll be okay, Samantha. I'll be back. I promise." His voice sounded steady and sure.

Finally, she nodded. Through the watery curtain around her, she watched as John disappeared. She prayed fervently for his safety as the wind whipped around and thunder shook the ground.

Only a man of character would go back to save the person who'd betrayed him. She only hoped that, in the process, Rich didn't stab him in the back again.

After a few minutes, John's blurry figured appeared pulling someone behind him. He deposited Rich at the tree across from her and he sagged there, nearly lifeless.

Samantha soaked in the man's expressionless face. "Is he okay?" she asked.

John nodded. "He's still breathing, just unconscious. He'll be fine."

John sat beside her and wrapped his arms around her, sheltering her from the storm.

Her heart burst with love. Here was a man who'd sacrifice himself for her safety. He'd go through discomfort and pain to give her a little more peace of mind. How could she not have seen this earlier?

She couldn't wait to tell him.

A gust of wind sent cold rain and leaves smattering into them.

They could do this. She'd survived Billy's threats over the past year. She'd survived *Billy*. A nor'easter wasn't going to take her out.

As lightning broke through the sky, she braced herself, knowing she could conquer anything with John by her side.

NINETEEN

The coast guard rescued Samantha, John and Rich three hours later. A small window of opportunity had broken in the storm, and the coast guard had seized the moment.

A helicopter took them back to the mainland, where they were taken to the hospital and examined by doctors.

That night, after they were released, they'd camped out at Nate and Kylie's place. Connor and Rusty were waiting for them there. They'd managed to catch the last ferry, right before the storm got bad.

Meanwhile, Rich had been arrested. The police were still piecing together everything, but it appeared that Billy had been in disguise as Agent Walsh. John suspected that he'd followed Kylie to the island and had fired the shots at Samantha that day. Samantha couldn't believe that, being a cop, he'd missed. But she was thankful that he had. Billy was also being investigated for Lisa's death.

The local detective had hinted that the FBI would be getting involved, and that it seemed there was a long list of crimes Billy was responsible for.

Because of Samantha's text message, Nate had alerted the authorities about the documents hidden in the safe-deposit box. Samantha had been cleared of all allegations, in both the death of her husband and Lisa.

In all of that craziness, John and Samantha hadn't had a moment to talk. Not to really talk.

With Connor asleep, Samantha closed the door behind her and stepped into the hallway. All was quiet in the house. Nate and Kylie had obviously gone to bed already.

John was waiting there, leaning against the wall with his phone in hand.

He held it up, a twinkle in his eyes.

He'd gotten her text message.

Her cheeks heated at the thought. If her life hadn't been on the line, she probably wouldn't have admitted those things to him. But she honestly didn't think she'd ever see him again.

She didn't regret sending it, though.

"John, I—"

Before she said anything else, John had closed the space between them in three long steps, and Samantha was in his arms. Their lips met, this time without any hesitation.

"I love you Samantha Rogers," he whispered. "I know it seems too early, too fast, but it's true. I love you."

"What about Alyssa?"

He shook his head. "I have to let it go and forgive myself. Alyssa would want that."

"When did you realize all of that?"

"A lot of things become clear when the life of someone you love is on the line. I didn't know how any of this would turn out, but I knew if I survived this, I had to stop letting the past hold me back."

Joy burst in her chest, spreading warmth all the way down to the tips of her fingers. "I love you, too. I'm so glad you were in the restaurant that evening when I decided I was going to leave. I'm so glad you told me about Smuggler's Cove."

"I'm glad you were crazy enough to give the island

a try." His fingers laced through hers and he pulled her closer. "Now that you've been officially cleared of the charges, will you be returning to Texas?"

She snuggled closer to him. "I was hoping I might still have a job on Smuggler's Cove. I'm a pretty good handy-woman, even if I do say so myself."

He grinned and brushed a stray hair from her face. "I'd say you're pretty good, too. I was hoping you might make your position on the island permanent."

"Hmm…" She tapped her chin playfully. "I'd definitely consider that."

John's eyes lost some of their sparkle for a moment. "What do you think Connor would say?"

"As long as he's with Rusty, he'll be fine. I think he's become pretty fond of you, too." She rested her hand on his chest.

A huge grin stretched across his face. "The feeling is mutual."

Their lips met in another kiss.

And somehow, all of the mistakes and messes of her past seemed to disappear and the promise of a bright new future loomed on the horizon.

* * * * *

Dear Reader,

Thank you for visiting the fictional Smuggler's Cove with me. The town is loosely based on Tangier Island in the Chesapeake Bay, a place where it truly does feel like time has stood still in many regards. I hope you enjoyed John and Samantha's story. When I first introduced John in *Keeping Guard,* I knew I wanted to tell his story one day.

I'm currently working on Ed Carter's story. Ed was first introduced in *High-Stakes Holiday Reunion.* I'm really enjoying his book, which is the second in the Smuggler's Cove series. It features a nurse with a secret, an ex-CIA operative, a creepy old house and a raging storm on a secluded island.

I hope you'll remember that there's someone we can trust throughout all of the storms raging in our lives, no matter how hopeless our circumstances may feel at times.

I love hearing from readers. You can find me at www.christybarritt.com. Be sure to sign up for my newsletter to get updates on my latest releases.

Many blessings,

Christy Barritt

Questions for Discussion

1. Would you like to live in a place like Smuggler's Cove? What would you like or dislike about it?

2. Have you ever been falsely accused like Samantha was? What feelings did you experience? How did you overcome the situation?

3. Samantha had to choose between paying for a crime she didn't commit or going on the run. Have you ever been between a rock and a hard place? How did you react? What advice would you give others in that place?

4. Is running away from your problems ever the right choice? Why or why not?

5. Why is facing our fears so difficult? When is a time in your life you've done something even though you were terrified?

6. Guilt can be a strong motivator for our decisions. John definitely struggled with the emotion after the death of his wife. How do you deal with guilt? How can we determine when our guilt is a sign that we've done something wrong or when guilt is an emotion that keeps us in bondage?

7. Samantha feels like every man in her life has let her down. Sometimes she projects those feelings onto God. How can we differentiate our disappointment in people from the unfailing love of our heavenly Father?

8. What prevents you from trusting people? Have you ever been hurt or let down after trusting someone? Did that affect your future relationships?

9. John gave up a secure job in order to follow his dreams and allow change in his life. Do you choose the safe and familiar or the new and unknown?

10. What's one thing in your life you'd like to change? Are there small ways you can go about implementing that change?

REQUEST YOUR FREE BOOKS!

2 FREE RIVETING INSPIRATIONAL NOVELS
PLUS 2 FREE MYSTERY GIFTS

Love Inspired®
SUSPENSE

YES! Please send me 2 FREE Love Inspired® Suspense novels and my 2 FREE mystery gifts (gifts are worth about $10). After receiving them, if I don't wish to receive any more books, I can return the shipping statement marked "cancel." If I don't cancel, I will receive 4 brand-new novels every month and be billed just $4.74 per book in the U.S. or $5.24 per book in Canada. That's a savings of at least 21% off the cover price. It's quite a bargain! Shipping and handling is just 50¢ per book in the U.S. and 75¢ per book in Canada.* I understand that accepting the 2 free books and gifts places me under no obligation to buy anything. I can always return a shipment and cancel at any time. Even if I never buy another book, the two free books and gifts are mine to keep forever.

123/323 IDN F5AC

Name	(PLEASE PRINT)
Address	Apt. #
City	State/Prov.	Zip/Postal Code
Signature (if under 18, a parent or guardian must sign)	

Mail to the **Harlequin®** Reader Service:
IN U.S.A.: P.O. Box 1867, Buffalo, NY 14240-1867
IN CANADA: P.O. Box 609, Fort Erie, Ontario L2A 5X3

**Are you a current subscriber to Love Inspired Suspense books
and want to receive the larger-print edition?
Call 1-800-873-8635 or visit www.ReaderService.com.**

* Terms and prices subject to change without notice. Prices do not include applicable taxes. Sales tax applicable in N.Y. Canadian residents will be charged applicable taxes. Offer not valid in Quebec. This offer is limited to one order per household. Not valid for current subscribers to Love Inspired Suspense books. All orders subject to credit approval. Credit or debit balances in a customer's account(s) may be offset by any other outstanding balance owed by or to the customer. Please allow 4 to 6 weeks for delivery. Offer available while quantities last.

Your Privacy—The Harlequin® Reader Service is committed to protecting your privacy. Our Privacy Policy is available online at www.ReaderService.com or upon request from the Harlequin Reader Service.
We make a portion of our mailing list available to reputable third parties that offer products we believe may interest you. If you prefer that we not exchange your name with third parties, or if you wish to clarify or modify your communication preferences, please visit us at www.ReaderService.com/consumerschoice or write to us at Harlequin Reader Service Preference Service, P.O. Box 9062, Buffalo, NY 14269. Include your complete name and address.

LIS13R

SPECIAL EXCERPT FROM

Love Inspired

*Get ready for a Big Sky wedding…or fifty! Here's a
sneak peek at
HIS MONTANA BRIDE by Brenda Minton,
part of the BIG SKY CENTENNIAL miniseries:*

"Bad news," Cord said. "That was the wedding coordinator. She's quitting."

"Ouch. So now what?"

"I'm not sure."

"With no coordinator to help, will you call off the wedding?" Katie asked.

"No." There was too much at stake. The town needed this wedding and the money it would bring in. They had a bridge in need of repairs and a museum they couldn't finish without more funds. "I'll just figure out how to pull off a wedding for fifty couples, maybe get some media attention for Jasper Gulch and hopefully not mess up anyone's life."

"I think you'll do just fine. Remember, it's all about the dress."

"How long are you going to be in town, Katie?" He placed a hand on her back and guided her up the sidewalk.

"I'm not sure. I'm supposed to be helping my sister, but she seems to have escaped and left me here." She sighed and glanced at him.

"Do you think that as long as you're here…"

They were standing in front of the massive wooden doors that led to the church. She had a slightly red nose from the cool morning air and her lips were tinted with pink gloss. As long as she was there, she could be a friend. That wasn't what he'd planned to say, but the thought framed itself as a question in his mind.

She was studying his face, waiting for him to finish.

"Maybe you could help me with this wedding?"

"I thought maybe you wanted me to run interference and keep the single women at bay. 'Hands off Cord Shaw,' that kind of thing." As she said it, somehow her palm came to rest on his shoulder as if they'd been friends forever.

It was the strangest and maybe one of the best feelings. It tangled him up and made him lose track of the reality that he was standing in front of the church. The door could open at any moment. And for the first time in years, a woman had made him feel at ease.

Can rancher Cord Shaw and Katie Archer pull off Jasper Gulch's latest centennial event without getting their hearts involved? Find out in
HIS MONTANA BRIDE by Brenda Minton,
available October 2014 from Love Inspired.

SPECIAL EXCERPT FROM

Love Inspired
SUSPENSE

Danger and love go hand in hand in the small town
of Wrangler's Corner. Read on for a sneak preview of
THE LAWMAN RETURNS by Lynette Eason,
the first book in this exciting new series from
Love Inspired Suspense.

Sheriff's deputy Clay Starke wheeled to a stop in front of
the beat-up trailer. He heard the sharp crack, and the side
of the trailer spit metal.

A shooter.

The woman on the porch careened down the steps and
bolted toward him. Terror radiated from her. He shoved
open the door to the passenger side. "Get in!"

Breathless, she landed in the passenger seat and slammed
the door. Eyes wide, she lifted shaking hands to push her
blond hair out of her eyes.

Clay got on his radio and reported shots fired.

He cranked the car and started to back out of the drive.

"No! We can't leave!"

"What?" He stepped on the brake. "Lady, if someone's
shooting, I'm getting you out of here."

"But I think Jordan's in there, and I can't leave without
him."

"Jordan?"

"A boy I work with. He called me for help. I'm worried
he might be hurt."

Clay put the car back in Park. "Then stay down and let
me check it out."

"But if you get out, he might shoot you."

He waited. No more shots. "Stay put. I think he might be gone."

"Or waiting for one of us to get out of the car."

True. He could feel her gaze on him, studying him, dissecting him. He frowned. "What is it?"

"You."

He shot a glance behind them, then let his gaze rove the area until he'd gone in a full circle and was once again looking into her pretty face. "What about me?"

Red crept into her cheeks. "You look so much like Steven. Are you related?"

He stilled, focusing in on her. "I'm Clay Starke. You knew my brother?"

"Clay? I'm Sabrina Mayfield."

Oh, wow. Sabrina Mayfield. "Are you saying the kid in there knows something about Steven's death?"

"I don't know what he's doing here, but he called me and said he thought he knew who killed Steven and he needed me to come get him."

A tingle of shock raced through Clay. Finally. After weeks with nothing, this could be the break he'd been looking for. "Then I want to know what he knows."

*Pick up THE LAWMAN RETURNS, available
October 2014 wherever
Love Inspired Suspense books are sold.*

Love Inspired SUSPENSE
RIVETING INSPIRATIONAL ROMANCE

AROUND-THE-CLOCK PROTECTOR

Despite the threats against her life, Danielle Barclay thinks having a bodyguard is unnecessary. Or at least that's what she tells herself before meeting Jake Rabb. A former Delta Force solider, Jake is used to rope-lining from helicopters into enemy territory–not following around a senator's daughter. The lovely deputy district attorney is as strong-willed as she is brave, especially when the escalating danger assures Jake that her stalker means business. As the attacks become personal, Danielle finally puts her trust–and her feelings–on the line with her defender. But how will Jake protect her if the stalker is closer than they think?

KEEPING WATCH
by
JANE M. CHOATE

Available October 2014 wherever
Love Inspired books and ebooks are sold.

Find us on Facebook at
www.Facebook.com/LoveInspiredBooks

LIS44629